OUTER BANKS

LIGHTS OUT

ALYSSA SHEINMEL

AMULET BOOKS

NEW YORK

Library of Congress Catalog Number for
the hardcover edition: 2021037688

Paperback ISBN 978-1-4197-5807-2

Text © 2021 Outer Banks TM/© Netflix
Book design by Brenda E. Angelilli
Illustrations by Matt Taylor

Published in paperback in 2022 by Amulet Books, an imprint of ABRAMS. Originally published in hardcover by Amulet Books in 2021. All rights reserved. No portion of this book may be reproduced, stored in a retrieval system, or transmitted in any form or by any means, mechanical, electronic, photocopying, recording, or otherwise, without written permission from the publisher.

Printed and bound in U.S.A
10 9 8 7 6 5 4 3 2

Amulet Books are available at special discounts when purchased in quantity for premiums and promotions as well as fundraising or educational use. Special editions can also be created to specification. For details, contact specialsales@abramsbooks.com or the address below.

Amulet Books® is a registered trademark of Harry N. Abrams, Inc.

ABRAMS The Art of Books
195 Broadway, New York, NY 10007
abramsbooks.com

CHAPTER 1

JOHN B

THE SECURITY GUARD ALMOST SAW ME, BUT JJ PULLED THE
back of my shirt and I ducked just in time. The four of us crouched in the
darkness as the guard drove past in his golf cart.

"Do you think the hotel has special golf carts just for security guards?" JJ
whispers. "Like, all tricked out with sirens like police cars?"

"Maybe," I answer, though I didn't see any special equipment on the cart
that passed us. Not that I had a chance to look that closely.

All four of us—JJ, Pope, Kiara, and me—stand and continue our trek across
the hotel's golf course.

Now that the security guard is out of earshot, JJ doesn't bother whispering. "Spring break sucks," he announces firmly.

JJ's not exactly a "look on the bright side" kind of guy. Trust me, there'd be
no point in telling him, *Hey, at least it's a week or two off school,* because it's not
like he cares about school anyhow. Or I could point out that the temperature
this afternoon got all the way up to 70 degrees (even though the average
high on the island this time of year is only 60), so we got to spend the day in

1

shorts and t-shirts, but he'd just point out that it's dropping down into the 40s overnight anyhow. Plus, then Kiara would launch into a lecture about climate change, and even though she's totally right about all that, Kiara's lectures aren't exactly a whole lotta fun. And we came out tonight looking for a good time.

Plus, the thing is, JJ's right. When you live in the OBX like we do, spring break *does* kind of suck.

You know those videos people post online, on some beautiful sandy beach with everyone in bathing suits and partying in the sunshine? Or maybe they're, I don't know, skiing on a mountaintop. Or staying at some luxury hotel getting spa treatments. Or skydiving or yacht racing or something in some exotic location. (Whatever rich people do in their spare time.) Anyway, those images come from places like *this*. The places where the rich folks—we call 'em Kooks—forget there are actual people who *live* in their vacation destinations all year round. Here in the Outer Banks, spring break means dozens of mainland Kooks breezing onto the island, filling the hotels, crowding the beaches, and taking up every seat at every restaurant. They clear out the local shops so there's no bait and tackle left for the rest of us to go fishing.

Then, two weeks later, they go home, leaving their (literal) messes behind for the locals to clean up.

So why argue with JJ when he's right? (It's hard enough arguing with him when he's wrong.) Spring break *sucks*. Or anyhow, it sucks for Pogues like us.

"At least you don't have to work the entire time," Kiara offers.

Kiara's definitely a "look on the bright side" type of person. Or maybe it's more that she believes that she can somehow *get* to the bright side, if only people would listen to what she has to say and learn everything she knows about inequality and environmental justice and that kind of thing.

She says all these partiers are bad for beach erosion, but they're also good for business—her parents' business. Her dad owns The Wreck, one of the most popular restaurants on the island, and spring break brings in a ton of customers. Ever since she was big enough to hold a tray, Kiara's had to work at the restaurant while everyone else is on vacation. Her parents could definitely hire someone else, but her dad thinks it's the sort of thing that builds character. Plus, he wants Kie to know all there is to know about running that restaurant. He thinks she's going to take over the place someday.

Of course, Kie has other plans. (Kie's also the type of person who always has other plans.) But her parents don't know their daughter wants to spend her life fighting for environmental justice, not serving platters of fresh oysters to rich folks who couldn't care less about stuff like that.

Kie tells me stuff she'd never tell her parents.

Not just me, I guess. Sure, I like to think she's closer to me than she is to JJ or Pope, but I bet JJ and Pope like to think the same thing. Kie's our best friend, but she's also a *girl*, and a really gorgeous, really cool girl. She's not even really a Pogue like the three of us.

I guess I should explain: Here at the OBX, the locals (and the spring breakers) are divided into two camps: the Kooks and the Pogues. The Kooks, like I said, are the rich families who spend their money at beachfront restaurants and hotels, and the Pogues are the ones who work at those restaurants and hotels. There's not really anything in between, not around here. On our island, you have either two jobs or two houses.

Anyway, the three of us—JJ, Pope, and me—act like we're not jealous or competitive about Kiara, but there's an unspoken thing in the air among us sometimes when Kie pulls her long hair up into a ponytail, exposing her soft neck, or emerges from the water in a wet bathing suit.

"At least your dad gave you tonight off," Pope offers, the voice of reason like always. Pope's not a bright side or dark side kind of guy—he just tells it like it is. He believes in truth and logic, that kind of stuff. So right now, he's pointing out that *yes, Kie has to work all through spring break,* but *she* does *have tonight off.* Which means the four of us get to hang out.

And maybe make some trouble, too.

"You sure you want to do this?" Pope asks, turning to me. I think sometimes he expects me to be the voice of reason, too. After all, I've been living on my own ever since my dad disappeared and I haven't burned the house down yet, so I must be doing something right.

My uncle Teddy is technically my guardian, but he's not exactly reliable. As in, I haven't seen or heard from him in weeks—he works in construction, and he splits whenever there's a building job to be had in some other city or town. As in, I'm living alone in the house where I used to live with my dad—no, wait: I still live there with my dad, he's just been gone. For a while.

4

But anyway, I've been on my own. And like I said, I haven't blown up the house yet, which is enough to make Pope think that I must be as mature as he is, which is why he's looking at me now, hoping I'll be the one to call off our latest plan.

Not a chance.

"Hell yeah, I wanna do this," I say. "Not about to let the Kooks have all the fun."

"Damn straight," JJ agrees.

What *is* our latest plan? It's pretty simple. Like I said, the hotels are packed to capacity with unfamiliar (Kook) faces for the next two weeks—families with whining kids, teenagers with their parents' credit cards. Which means hotel security already has its hands full looking for toddlers who wandered off when their parents were busy getting shit-faced, or trying to keep drunk Kook teens from diving into the freezing pools that are only open for show. Which means that four innocent Pogues like us have an opportunity to waltz right in without anyone noticing, lift some booze from the hotel bar or a for-gotten room service cart or whatever they have at those places (Kiara stayed at a nice hotel with her family in California last summer, so she knows how hotels work better than the rest of us), and party like it's, well, spring break, on our terms.

Why did Kie stay at a fancy hotel last summer? Like I said, even though she hangs out with us, she's *technically* a Kook. Her family lives in Figure 8, not on the Cut, which is the south side of the island where JJ, Pope, and I live. Kie even went to the Kook school for a year. But Kiara dislikes the Kooks as much as the rest of us and insists that she's a Pogue through and through.

That's why the four of us are currently dressed in shades of black and gray, sneaking across the golf course attached to the island's nicest hotel. I mean, go big or go home, right? If we're going to do this, we're going to do it at the *best* place, the sort of place where four Pogues wouldn't be caught dead.

JJ's got the hood of his sweatshirt pulled up over his blond hair. Kiara's wearing dark blue jeans with a black long-sleeved shirt on top. Pope showed up with a white t-shirt on over his jeans. I'd guessed he wouldn't really get it about stealth mode, so I brought an extra black shirt just in case and made him put it on over his white shirt before we stepped foot onto the hotel's perfectly manicured golf course.

"All we gotta do is get in and get out," JJ says. He's still wearing the shorts he had on this afternoon—when it was sunny and warm—and I can tell he's trying not to let us see that he's freezing now that the sun's gone down. JJ doesn't like to show weakness.

The golf course wraps around the hotel like a castle moat, but as we get closer to the main building, the silence of the empty course is taken over by a clamor of voices. Soon, we can see the hotel deck—there's a bright, shiny pool even though it's too cold to swim. At the far end of the pool is a hot tub that is full of littlish kids even though it's after ten. (I guess even rich parents don't care about bedtime on vacation.)

A bunch of adults—the kids' parents?—are milling around, fancy-looking drinks in their hands. Behind the pool is an elevated deck—the hotel restaurant—and a bunch of tables with heat lamps scattered among them so that people can sit outside regardless of the cold. Almost every table is occupied by a family—two parents, their daughters and sons, everyone clean and bright and smiling and dressed up.

"This doesn't even look like fun," I whisper, and I half mean it. At some of the tables there are teenagers sitting with their parents. Is that really how they want to spend their spring break, hanging out with their parents? Once we get out of here and back to my place, there will be no adults to tell us we're too young for anything, no Kiara's dad to tell her to get to work, no Pope's parents asking about his latest homework assignment, and definitely no JJ's dad getting into one of his moods.

I miss my dad, but I'd be lying if I said there weren't *some* advantages to living on your own.

I notice Sarah Cameron (local Kook princess) sitting at one of the tables with her parents and her brother. Her long, always-a-little-bit-messy blond hair is pulled into a ponytail. I already knew the Camerons weren't leaving the OBX for spring break because I work for Mr. Cameron—Ward—maintaining his yacht. Ward is smiling at all the tourists like he's the mayor or the island's official welcoming committee, but Sarah looks bored. Not that I know her so well that I can read the expression on her face, but the "bored teenager stuck with her parents" look is pretty universal.

"So much for stealth mode," Kiara whispers.

"What do you mean?" I ask.

"We don't exactly fit in in our current outfits." Kiara points to a group of middle-aged Kook women wearing long floral-print dresses with wedge sandals. They look freezing, like they didn't bother checking the weather before they packed their bags to head to the OBX. Or maybe they just thought, *Beach, island*, and assumed it was tropical even though the Carolina coast in March is obviously not. Sarah Cameron, at least—a local like us—is dressed weather-appropriately just like we are. (Well, except for JJ in his shorts.) Most of the men are wearing a variation on the exact same outfit: khaki pants, button-down shirt, navy blazer, striped tie. I wonder if their conversations are as dull as their clothes.

"Hey, Kie," I try. "You know how to fit in with the Kooks, right? Couldn't you just go right up to the bar and order a bunch of drinks, tell them to charge it to your room or something?"

Kie looks at me with daggers in her eyes. She hates when any of us remind her of her Kook status. I grin because I know she'll do whatever it takes to prove she's one of us, not one of them.

"I have a better idea," Kie says, pulling off her black shirt (she's wearing a t-shirt underneath) and tying it around her shoulders. She tucks her t-shirt into her jeans and pulls her hair into a tight bun at the nape of her neck. She doesn't look as fancy as the girls in dresses down there, but she can definitely fit in when she wants to.

"Follow my lead," she says, and strides onto the deck like she owns the place.

JJ, Pope, and I exchange a look, but we follow. As we pass the Camerons' table, I hear Sarah complaining about spending spring break at home.

"Look around," Ward, her dad, says. "People go to great lengths to spend spring break here."

"Topper's family went to *Vail* this weekend, Dad." Topper is Sarah's asshole boyfriend. "And everyone else is gone for two whole weeks! Can't we go somewhere just for a couple of days?"

"You don't even know how to ski," Ward points out reasonably.

"*Snowboard*," Sarah corrects, "and that is *not* the point."

I shake my head. Rich people problems are weird. Sarah catches me looking and raises an eyebrow, but she doesn't mention me to Ward and the rest of her family, or ask what I'm doing at a place like this. She knows as well as anyone that my friends and I don't exactly belong here.

"Told you I didn't need this," Pope says, pulling at the neckline of the black shirt I lent him.

I shrug. "Whatever. It got us across the golf course, didn't it?"

CHAPTER 2

JJ

KOOKS HAVE NO CLUE HOW TO PARTY. I MEAN, THEY HAVE all the money in the world, but they waste so much time being, I don't know, *civilized*. Here they are, on vacation, and they're just sitting around in their fancy clothes and expensive jewelry, posing like they're mannequins in a store window instead of actual people having actual *fun*.

On the hotel deck, there's a maze of tables and heating lamps filled with middle-aged folks and their kids looking practically comatose as they sip their expensive wine—the middle-aged folks, not the kids—and stare out at the ocean, which, I'm sorry, it's dark out, you can't actually *see* the water. I mean, this hotel is right on the beach, so you could probably hear the roar of the waves or something if the people milling around would shut up for two seconds.

It's almost enough to make you feel sorry for them.

Almost.

Actually, nah, not even close.

In the summer, out-of-town tourist Kooks crawl all over the island, and they're pretty easy targets. I mean, they're on vacation, they just want a good time. I lost count of how many out-of-town Kook girls I made out—and then some—with last summer. But for some reason, tonight, none of this looks like a good time.

It looks more like a waste of time.

Kiara leads the way past the empty pool and the crowded hot tub, onto the deck, straight into the lobby, and toward the elevators. The lobby has literal crystal chandeliers hanging down from vaulted ceilings, and the floors are made of bright, shiny marble arranged into an elaborate flowery pattern. A group of women walk past us, heels clicking against the floor. My sneakers squeak with each step I take.

"Where are we going?" John B whispers to Kie, his lips right up close to her ear, which is totally unnecessary. I mean, I can hear him from here and he's not pressing his mouth to my ear, but whatever, any excuse to get close to her, I guess.

"I have a plan," Kiara promises. We crowd into the elevator and she hits *B*, and the elevator descends to the basement.

"Wait here," she says with a wink, and disappears down the hall.

The basement of this hotel is nothing like the lobby upstairs, all marble floors and bright lights. Overhead, there are dim fluorescent bulbs, and the walls are cinder blocks painted dark blue.

Up ahead, there's an enormous bucket on wheels that looks like it's filled with dirty sheets and a couple of discarded room service trolleys. I head over and look at the uneaten food the Kooks upstairs left behind. There's a bottle of red wine that's only about two-thirds empty. I take a swig. It tastes terrible.

"You know, John B," I say, "when you said you wanted to sneak into this place, I didn't think you meant hanging out in the basement."

"What do you think, boys?" Kiara calls out from down the hall. I don't even recognize her at first. She's wearing a maid's uniform—black short sleeves with a white apron sewn into the front. Kie spins around like she's a supermodel.

"Where'd you get that?" John B asks.

Kiara grins. "Laundry room."

"You're wearing someone's dirty clothes?" Pope asks, looking grossed out.

"What, you thought the shirt I lent you was clean?" John B winks.

"I knew it smelled!" Pope shouts.

"Shh, you guys, you're gonna blow my cover," Kiara says, but she's laughing.

"Kie," I say, "no one is gonna believe you work here." The uniform is wrinkled and at least two sizes too big.

Kiara shakes her head. "You're assuming rich folks actually *look* at the people serving them. Trust me, after years at The Wreck, I know better." The Wreck is a magnet for Kooks and tourists, which means it's a magnet

13

for their money, too. Sometimes we joke that her dad should have two menus: one for the locals with the real prices, and other one for the tourists with inflated prices.

"Okay," John B says, "but what's the point? How does you dressing up like a maid get us free booze?"

I don't care about the point. And not just 'cause I'd follow Kie wherever she told me to go. And that's not because she's a girl or because she's hot—which she is, but that's not what I'm getting at. I'd follow John B and Pope anywhere, too. But I mean, I don't need to know the details of Kie's plan because I'm up for whatever. It's spring break, and the Kooks don't deserve to keep all the fun—or what they think passes for fun, anyhow—for themselves.

Plus, the grin on Kie's face tells me that whatever she's got planned, it's gonna be a blast. She tosses John B and Pope white button-down shirts and black vests and tells them to change.

"What about me?" I ask.

"You're wearing shorts, JJ. Rich people might not look closely, but they'll notice someone *that* out of uniform."

I guess she has a point. I mean, Pope and John B are wearing jeans, but at least their pants are dark blue, unlike my khaki cargo shorts. Still, I hate being left out.

"Follow me," Kiara says, grabbing one of the room service trolleys before stepping into the elevator. She pushes the button for the highest floor—seven. When the elevator doors open, we're facing another long hallway that's nothing like the hall in the basement. This is warmly lit with those tacky lamps along the walls that are supposed to look like candles, complete with fake plastic wax drips. There's a thick carpet on the floor, so at least my sneakers won't squeak.

"So," Kie says, dropping her voice, stopping and leaning against the cart. "Hotels like this have mini-fridges full of food and drinks, and they charge you, like, twelve dollars for a Diet Coke. But they also stock those fridges with teeny-tiny bottles of wine and beer and liquor, too. *Pocket*-sized," she adds with a wink. "So we just have to get into one of the rooms."

"Okay, but how exactly are we going to do that?" John B asks.

"Turndown service!" Kie explains gleefully. "When my parents and I were in California last year, the maids would knock on our doors every night to, like, set up the room for sleeping. They'd close the blinds and rearrange the pillows on the bed. So, all we have to do is knock on a few doors. A lot of these rooms are empty now, so we obviously can't get inside—real turndown service people have their own keys—but we just need a few people to open up so we can get inside."

"And rearrange their pillows?" I ask.

Kie looks at me witheringly. I fold my arms across my chest as she continues. "Pope and John B will go inside while I distract the guests in the doorway. And then one of you can fluff the pillows and close the blinds while the other one cleans out the minibar. Just hide whatever you take in your pockets before you leave."

Pope says, "Yeah, but won't the people in those rooms get charged for whatever we take?"

"Maybe." Kie shrugs. "Half of them are so rich that they won't even notice the charges, and the other half will insist they never touched whatever we took and complain until the hotel takes it off their bills. The hotel's already overcharging, so the loss won't hurt it or anything."

"Okay, but if they're mini-bottles, won't we need a ton of them?" I ask.

"This place has, like, a zillion rooms. If we can pull this off in just one room on every floor, we'll get away with—"

"A shitload of liquor," I supply.

"Spring break for everybody!" Kiara throws her arms overhead like she won something, though she keeps her voice low. Sometimes I think Kie likes Kooks even less than I do. I mean, I thought we'd just sneak behind the bar downstairs and grab a bottle, but her plan is so much more elaborate.

Pope shakes his head. "This is a bad idea. We could get into trouble."

"Oh, are you worried about a little bit of trouble?" I make my voice high-pitched, faking concern. In my regular voice, I say, "You worry too much, Pope. Anyone ever tell you that?"

"Just you," Pope answers. "And you think anyone who worries about anything at all is worrying too much." He punches my shoulder.

Kiara leads us to an alcove in the center of the hallway with an ice machine and a vending machine.

"You stay here, JJ," she instructs. I think she feels bad that I don't really have much of a role to play, so she adds, "You keep an eye out and warn us if any real hotel staff are coming."

Kie knocks on one door, then another and another. There's no answer; I guess whoever's staying in these rooms is downstairs on the deck or by the pool area or whatever.

And I'm sorry, but this is boring. There's nothing interesting about knocking on doors and getting no answer. I'm about to call it when an old man actually answers a door. He's wearing a fluffy white bathrobe with the hotel's name embroidered on the front.

"Turndown service," Kiara says cheerfully. John B and Pope slip inside while Kiara keeps the old man in the doorway, asking where he's from and how he's enjoying his stay. I guess after all these years of working at The Wreck, she knows how to make small talk with Kooks and tourists.

After a few minutes, John B and Pope come back into the hallway. I can tell they're trying not to laugh. As soon as the old man closes the door behind him, the three of them make a beeline for the alcove where I'm hiding. Pope starts pacing back and forth, like he's convinced he got caught even though they pulled it off without a hitch.

"Here," John B says, filling my pockets with tiny bottles of alcohol. "I need to make space for the next room."

"Ready to go again?" Kie says, heading down the hall to the elevator.

The bottles in my pockets make a satisfying clink when I walk. "Hell yeah," I say.

On the sixth floor, no one answers the door.

On the fifth floor, Kiara gets an answer on the second door she knocks on, but the hotel guests say they don't want turndown service.

But we have better luck on the fourth and third floors.

By the time we press the elevator button for the second floor, my pockets are so full of teeny-tiny bottles that I think my shorts are going to fall off from holding all the extra weight.

When the elevator doors open on the second floor, though, we come face-to-face with a couple of Kooks instead of an empty hallway. Like, a literal couple—a boy and a girl holding hands. They look like they're about our age, but they're dressed just like those old farts down by the pool.

The guy is tall, with dark hair that looks like he spent several hours and three bottles of hair gel trying—and failing—to get it to frame his face perfectly. The girl has perfectly straight brown hair that goes down to her chest.

Kiara puts her face down, pushing the trolley in front of her. "Excuse me," she says softly.

"This is my floor," I say, squeezing past her, trying to look like I have a room here and it's just a coincidence that I was on an elevator with the housekeeping staff. I don't look back, but I can hear Kie and Pope and John B getting off the elevator, too.

"Oh hey," the girl says, and for a second I think she knows what we're up to, but then I turn back and see that she's talking to Kiara. I notice the girl has light brown eyes and a smattering of freckles across the bridge of her nose.

"My boyfriend and I are planning a party in our room in a couple days. Half our school is here for spring break. Could you help us with, you know, catering and that sort of thing?"

"Catering?" Kiara echoes.

"Yeah, I mean, we know we can get food from the hotel, but let's face it, they charge twice as much here as anywhere else—"

"Savannah, we don't have to worry about that sort of thing."

The girl—Savannah, I guess—blushes when her boyfriend interrupts her. Must be nice to have so much money that you know you're getting ripped off but you still don't care.

"I just meant," the girl says quickly, "it might be nice to get food from someplace local, you know, instead of all these touristy places."

"Honey," the guy says, "the touristy places are the *good* places. Everything else around here is a dump."

Kiara bristles, but she's not about to blow her cover on a stupid Kook saying stupid shit. Kie was right about one thing—rich people don't really look at the people who serve them. This guy hasn't looked at her once. He holds his gaze somewhere above her head.

"You're right. I'm sorry," the girl says. She rubs her bare arms like she's

19

cold. She's wearing one of those dresses that ties behind her head—a halter dress. Not nearly warm enough for this weather, though I'm wearing shorts so who am I to judge? The girl says, "I'm gonna go back to the room real quick, grab a sweater."

I realize that I must look like a creep, listening to their conversation, so I start walking down the hallway, pretending I have a room at the other end. Hopefully this girl and her obnoxious boyfriend will get back on the elevator before I get to the end of the hall. And hopefully that guy won't notice the way my shorts click and clink with every step I take.

But even if he does, I'm pretty sure I'd have no trouble outrunning a Kook like him.

CHAPTER 3

JOHN B

THE KOOKS DISAPPEAR INTO THE ELEVATOR, AND KIARA'S about to start knocking on doors when I notice it.

"Kie," I whisper, even though it's just the four of us in the hallway now. "That girl—"

"Savannah," Kiara supplies. I shrug.

"She left her door open. I mean, she closed it after she got her sweater, but it didn't latch." I push on the door of her room—206—and it opens.

JJ, Pope, Kiara, and I slip inside, leaving the room service trolley in the hallway. The room looks exactly like the others we've been in: big bed, huge TV, mini-fridge built into the cabinets. JJ is so focused on getting to the fridge that he doesn't notice the shiny silver bucket filled with ice on the bedside table.

I grab the bottle from the bucket. "Mo-et," I read.

"It's pronounced *Mo-ay*," Kiara says. "It's champagne." She grins as she takes the bottle from me. JJ drops onto the bed and pulls out one of the tiny bottles he's collected in his shorts, opening it. Pope sits beside him, popping macadamia nuts into his mouth.

"What?" Pope says, when he catches me looking. "We didn't say we could *only* take booze."

JJ rolls his eyes and reaches for the remote control, making himself comfortable.

"Man," he says running his hands across the bed, "I've never felt sheets this soft."

"I think we should get going," I say slowly.

"What's the rush?" JJ says. "It's not like that girl's going to need *another* sweater."

But almost as soon as he says it, I hear voices in the hallway outside. It's that girl and her boyfriend again. Sounds like the girl realized that after she got herself a sweater, she didn't close the door all the way, and she's coming back to make sure it's locked.

"Oh shit," JJ says, throwing the remote to the floor like it's hot. "What are we going to do?"

I stand by the door. "I think they're still down the hall. By the elevators maybe?"

Kie says, "Let's just make a run for it."

JJ breaks in: "And go where? If they're at the elevators—"

"There's a stairwell at the other end of the hallway. In case of fire."

Pope asks, "What if an alarm goes off when we open the door to the stairs?"

Kie looks at the three of us like we're nuts. "While you guys stand here debating the logistics, I'm getting out." She throws the door open and starts running in the opposite direction of the elevators.

"Don't have to tell me twice," I say, running after her. I hear JJ and Pope behind me.

"Hey!" the guy's voice shouts, but none of us look back. "That's our room!"

Kiara gets to the stairwell first. (She's the only one who doesn't have pockets full of booze slowing her down.) She holds open the door for JJ, Pope, and me (no alarm goes off), and we dash through and run down the stairs.

I think we're in the clear, but then I hear footsteps on the stairs behind us.

"Shit, that guy is following us!" I shout as Kie flies out the door and right smack into the middle of the crowded lobby.

"Come on," she says urgently, reaching back to take my hand. I squeeze. Her hand is cold from holding the icy champagne bottle. I follow her through the crowd of Kooks back to the deck and the pool, JJ and Pope on our heels.

Behind us, a voice shouts out, "Security!" Much to my surprise, it's not the guy's voice but the girl's. *She's* the one who ran after us down the stairs. "Those kids broke into our room!"

Kiara is still wearing her maid's uniform, and Pope and I have on our vests and button-downs. In the fancy lobby, it makes us stand out, not blend in. Plus, the way we're running doesn't exactly make us inconspicuous, either.

There's a rent-a-cop standing by the glass double doors from the lobby to the deck. He looks up in surprise—guess stuff like this doesn't usually happen here—but before he can block the door, Sarah Cameron is standing beside him, pointing in the opposite direction.

"That's lucky," JJ pants as he shoots through the door, Pope and Kiara at his heels. I pause just long enough to see Sarah wink at me, but there's no time to wonder why she helped us.

Kie and I run down the stairs off the side of the deck back onto the golf course. Ahead of us, JJ skips the stairs altogether and literally dives off the side of the deck, Pope at his heels. I hear JJ cursing and I realize that some of the bottles in his shorts shattered.

My side hurts from running so hard and so fast, but I don't stop. The farther we go onto the golf course, the darker it gets and the less chance we have of getting caught. I don't know how far or how long we've been running before Kiara finally stops on one of the greens. The little flag that marks the hole is bright white and visible in the darkness.

"I think we lost them," she says, breathing hard. She unzips her maid's uniform, revealing her own clothes hiding underneath.

Kie pulls her phone out of her pocket and turns on the flashlight, then bursts out laughing. I turn and see JJ and Pope running up behind us—JJ in nothing but his boxers, his soaking wet shorts balled up in his fist.

"What happened to your shorts?" I ask, though I can barely keep a straight face.

"They fell off! I was running so fast that they just shimmied right down my legs."

Pope says, "More like they were soaked from all that booze and you were tripping all over yourself."

A shadow falls over JJ's face. He prefers his version of events to Pope's. Kiara cuts the tension by popping the cork of the champagne bottle.

"Shh!" Pope hisses. "We don't want them to hear us."

Kie raises the bottle to her lips and takes a sip. "Believe me, Pope. People that rich aren't going to run this far for one bottle of champagne."

"I don't know, that Kook girl seemed pretty pissed," I say.

"Savannah," Kie corrects. "Her name was Savannah."

"Whatever her name was, she seemed determined to catch us," Pope insists. "We should get out of here. Even if she doesn't come after us, one of those golf-cart security guards might find us."

Kiara makes a show of tiptoeing across the green toward the edge of the golf course, where we parked my van earlier tonight. I get behind the wheel and we drive to the beach.

"It's freezing!" JJ shouts when I park. We get out of the van and trudge toward the water. The wind whips my hair into my eyes. I pull the bandana from around my neck and twist it around my forehead to keep my hair out of my face.

"Imagine how much warmer you'd be if only you had pants," I say.

Kie doubles over laughing, then passes the bottle of Moet to me. I've never had champagne before. The bubbles make me snort. "*This* is what Kooks drink?" I ask, before passing the bottle to Pope, who passes it to JJ.

"I've said it before, and I'll say it again," JJ says. "Kooks have no idea how to have fun. I mean, they come all the way to the OBX from whatever cities they live in, and they're all crowded into that hotel like ants when they could be out here on the beach."

"Thought you were freezing," Pope points out.

"I'd rather freeze out here than keep warm under those stupid heat lamps. I mean, they may as well just stay wherever they came from if that's how they're going to spend their vacation."

"What do you think is worse," I ask, "Kook tourists or Kook locals?"

"We need a different name for them," Kie says instead of answering.

"For who?"

"The Kook tourists." She passes the bottle to JJ, who winks at her like they're sharing a secret. Kie rolls her eyes. JJ is forever flirting with Kie, but she always shuts it down. Besides, there's an unspoken no-Pogue-on-Pogue macking agreement among the four of us.

"I know what we should call them," JJ says, making a face at the taste of the champagne. "Morons." He passes the bottle to Pope, who shakes his head. Pope doesn't like to get shit-faced like the rest of us. He's too busy thinking about the next day's homework assignment, even on spring break.

Suddenly, Kie's face lights up. "That's it!" she says.

"What's it?" I echo.

"Tour-ons!" Kiara shouts gleefully. "Tourists who are morons. Tourons!"

"It's a portmanteau," Pope says, and the three of us look at him like he's speaking gibberish. Pope rolls his eyes. "It's a word that results from blending two or more words, or parts of words. Like how *smog* is *smoke* and *fog*, or *spork* is *spoon* and *fork*. A portmanteau."

"Dude, we're making fun of asshole Kooks, not studying for the SATs," JJ says.

"Pope can't help it," Kie says, putting her arm around Pope's shoulders. "He's always studying for something. He dreams of the Periodic Table."

"I do not," Pope says, but he doesn't shrug off Kie's arm.

"What's that word again?" I ask.

"Tourons!" Kie supplies.

"No, the other word. The word for what it is."

"Portmanteau," Pope says.

"Well, I think you're a Pope-manteau," I say.

"That's a portmanteau, too!" Kie shouts. "Popemanteau the portmanteau!"

The four of us double over laughing, practically rolling across the sand.

✳ ✳ ✳

Later, once the champagne has worn off, I drop Kie at home first, since her house is closest to the hotel. I drive slowly along the beach toward the Cut. At first, we're passing mansions and family compounds, but I know the farther south I go, the smaller the houses will get. It's so cold now that I can see my breath, but I keep the windows rolled down so I can smell the ocean while I drive. Like my dad, I don't think I could ever live anywhere that wasn't close to the water. I'd rather be *on* the water—fishing, surfing, swimming—than pretty much anywhere else. We're alike that way.

Beside me, Pope's half asleep, his head leaning against the window; JJ's smoking in the back seat. Some of the mansions I pass are totally dark because the people who own these homes are only here for a few weeks out of the year in the summertime; they spend most of the year on the mainland. I wonder why they're not here for spring break, but maybe they have more houses in other vacation destinations. Maybe they're backpacking across Europe or skiing—excuse me, *snowboarding*, I think, remembering Sarah Cameron's conversation with her dad—in Aspen or whatever the hell rich people do when they're not crowding our island.

I wonder why Sarah distracted that security guard so we could make a—sorta—clean getaway. Maybe she felt sorry for us, a bunch of Pogues who can't afford to buy their own booze. Maybe she was just bored, stuck at home with her family while her boyfriend's out of town. Sarah and Kie used to be best friends (for a hot minute in ninth grade, anyway), before they became total enemies. But still, maybe Sarah was helping us because the part of her who used to be friends with Kie wanted to help Kie stay out of trouble.

Or maybe Sarah was jealous, because it looked like we were having so much more fun than she was. Maybe helping us out was her way of joining in the fun, just for a second.

We drive past a house that's completely lit up. The Kooks who live there must be hosting their friends and family from the mainland for spring break, filling up their guesthouses and pool houses and maybe even their docked boats with their rich friends. I wonder if the Camerons' house will be full of guests before break is over. If her boyfriend, Topper, is only away for the weekend, maybe he'll come back home so they can spend the rest of spring break together. I wonder if Sarah will still look bored.

JJ coughs in the back seat, startling Pope. The two of them start bickering, but I sigh as we pass another dark house. Imagine having a house this huge, right on the nicest stretch of the beach, and not wanting to be here all the time, every minute. But even with all these empty houses, spring break means the island will be overflowing with Kooks one way or another.

That's the thing about Kooks. They act like they're breathing rarified air, but somehow there's still a never-ending supply of them.

CHAPTER 4

JJ

I'M SHIVERING BY THE TIME I GET BACK TO THE SOUTH SIDE of the island—the Cut, where John B and Pope and I live.

I toss my soaking wet, sticky shorts onto the floor and tiptoe into the kitchen. Dad's snoring on the couch. The lights are off, but the TV's on in front of him, giving off enough light that I can grab the peanut butter out of the cabinet. I stick my fingers into the jar.

"Use a knife, dammit," Dad says, and I nearly jump out of my skin. I thought he was passed out, or at least asleep.

Dad stomps into the kitchen and grabs the peanut butter. I lick my fingers.

"You're disgusting," Dad says. He rips a paper towel from the roll on the kitchen counter and tosses it to me. I wipe the peanut butter from my hands even though I'm still hungry.

"You smell like a distillery," Dad adds, wrinkling his nose.

"So do you," I mumble, but Dad doesn't hear me. Or anyway, he doesn't act like he does.

I don't actually know what a distillery smells like, but I know my dad is smashed.

"Look at you," Dad continues, though he doesn't. I mean, he doesn't look at me. He reaches over me to put the peanut butter jar back into the cabinet. "Already drinking at your age, and god knows what else." Dad shakes his head like he's disgusted. "You'll never amount to anything acting the way you do."

I know I should keep quiet. But I never do. "Guess I'm following in my old man's footsteps, huh?"

Dad slaps me across the face. My head whips back, crashing against the cabinet behind me. My teeth smack together.

"I didn't drink when I was your age," Dad says. He walks back to the couch and sits, his gaze returning to the TV like all he did was rub his eyes or scratch his balls, not smack his son. "In fact," he says, and he smiles a little bit, "I don't think I actually drank much at all before you came along."

It's bullshit. I *know* it's bullshit. No way was Dad the picture of sobriety before I was born. But it's not like my mom's around to tell me anything about how Dad used to be.

Dad continues: "But a man needs something to calm his nerves, living with such a disappointment, day after day."

I wish he'd shut up and go back to hitting me.

I stomp into my room.

"You clean up that mess," Dad calls after me. I'm not sure if he means the kitchen—which is always a mess—or my sticky shorts on the floor, but I don't turn back to find out. I slam the door shut behind me, but it still feels like he's too close, like I can still hear his voice in my ears.

My room and that fancy hotel room are so different, it's like they don't exist on the same planet, let alone the same island. The bed at the hotel was the biggest one I've ever seen, propped up on a platform, facing an enormous flat-screen TV. The mini-fridge wasn't even a mini-fridge at all—I mean, it was a fridge, but it was built into the cabinet beneath the TV so that it didn't distract from the furniture or whatever. I bet Dad doesn't even know that fridges like that exist. I didn't.

I shake my head as if I can shake *him*—Dad's voice, his words, his slap—out of my head. I rub my hands over my face, and when I drop them I see that there's blood on my palms—I must have bit my lip when he slapped me. I didn't even notice.

I open my door and jog out of the house, into the yard. I breathe in deeply, but the air is so thin and cool that it's hard to catch my breath. Somehow, though, I'm not cold anymore. I feel like I'm on fire.

Lit up in the darkness, our house looks like a shack compared to the hotel, with its stocked mini-fridges and twinkling lights and whatever. Crap. It's not just the room upstairs that was so much nicer. Even the *basement* of that place was nicer than our house.

But when I think about the hotel, I think about the families in the lobby, eating together in the restaurant. Sure, it didn't look like much fun—how is anything that *civilized* actually fun?—but it did look . . . I don't know. *Peaceful.* Like whoever those people were, and however boring their lives are, they weren't going to go home to a dump of a house and a shitty father like mine.

They say money can't buy happiness, but I say that's bullshit. Rich people live in nice places—they have maids and housekeepers to clean up their messes. Rich wives and moms don't leave their husbands and sons in search of something better because they already have whatever the *better* things are—the nice house, the picture-perfect family.

I can still see them, all those rich families sitting on the deck at that hotel—dads who come home after work in suits and ties and ask their kids about their days and take them out back to play baseball instead of watching TV like a drunken zombie.

I pace across the yard, stopping to shadowbox every couple steps.

Screw it. Screw those rich assholes. Screw them for showing up on our island, for crowding our spaces with their fancy cars and stupid dresses and high heels, and screw their fancy champagne that tastes like piss.

I hate spring break.

I hate being here when this island is crowded with Kook tourists.

Morons.

Tourons.

The new word doesn't make me laugh this time.

Every time I leave the house, I'm faced with Kooks everywhere I turn, but if I stay home I'm stuck with my dad. I stomp across the yard and climb into the hammock. It won't be the first time I've slept out here instead of going inside with Dad. The tourists wouldn't be caught dead on this part of the island, so at least I'm free from them here.

But when I close my eyes, I see them all over again.

All those rich families, so pleased with themselves for, I don't know, breathing the island air.

Don't they know that Pogues like me are breathing it, too?

Probably not. Like Kiara said, rich people don't notice people like us. Those tourists are completely oblivious to the fact that we actually live here. They don't care that they're taking up space that belongs to *us*, the people who're here all year round, the people whose families have lived on these islands for generations, like mine.

Local Kooks aren't any better. Their kids go to boarding school on the mainland, and then they jet off to New York City or Los Angeles or Paris or Rome any time they feel like it.

But they never stay gone.

They keep coming back. Crowding this island with their mansions and yachts and fancy SUVs, taking up every table at places like The Wreck, clearing out the shelves at Pope's dad's store, Heyward's. Expecting the rest of us to get out of their way when they walk down the street, like they're royalty or something.

They think they're so much better than the rest of us.

What do they know?

It's easy to be *better* when you don't have any problems.

CHAPTER 5

JOHN B

I HOLD MY BREATH FOR A SECOND BEFORE I GO INSIDE OUR house, an old fish shack on the marsh that Dad named the Chateau. It happens—this feeling—every time I approach the house. Just for a second, part of me thinks maybe, just maybe, Dad will be home. Maybe he'll be lounging on the couch in the living room drinking a beer, waiting for me so he can tell me the truth about where he's been all this time. Or maybe he'll be in his office—it's locked shut with a padlock now—but maybe this time his office door will be open, and he'll be working behind his desk, poring over his nautical maps, too busy and too distracted to talk to me, but still—*home*.

Or maybe he'll be waiting in my room, sitting on the edge of my bed, so we can finish the conversation we started before he left (the *fight* we had before he left), and I'll get to apologize for calling him a bad father for leaving me all the time, and he'll accept my apology while promising to be a better father from now on. Promising to stick around. Promising never to disappear like this ever again.

Dad's been gone for about six months, searching for something about a shipwreck—he never told me the details. Three months after he disappeared, the authorities wanted to declare him "presumed dead," but I refused to sign the papers. I wasn't about to give up. Dad raised me on stories of shipwrecks and unsurvivable storms. When I was little, the bedtime stories Dad told were dozens of tales of sailors who turned up after years—not months!—when their loved ones thought they were lost at sea. They got back home and their families and friends had already moved on. Like, their wives remarried, their homes were sold, their belongings auctioned off. I'm not letting that happen to my dad.

Not that my mom remarrying would be much of a problem, since she split when I was three. Now, she lives almost all the way across the country, in Colorado. When I picture Colorado (where I've never been, by the way, it's not like she's invited me to visit) I imagine a landlocked state covered in mountains and snow, the exact opposite of home. Like Mom didn't want just distance from Dad and me, but to live in a climate as different from marshes and sand and sun as humanly possible.

Of course, when I go inside, the house is empty. It looks exactly like it did when I left a few hours ago. There are school books scattered on the coffee table from the last time I took them home from my locker, fully intending to do my homework, just like I used to, but nothing really holds my interest lately. Nothing seems important, with my dad missing. So now I'm failing history, and while I've never been a straight A student, I've never actually gotten an F before. There's the same sour milk in the fridge, the same dirty dishes in the sink, the same empty pizza box on the coffee table surrounded by half-empty soda cans. Not only is my dad nowhere to be found, but my uncle and supposed guardian isn't here, either. Sometimes JJ stays over when he can't stand being in his own place, and even though he somehow makes a mess the instant he steps foot inside, it's still better than being alone. I think I must spend more time alone than anyone I've ever met.

Kooks are never alone. They travel in packs around the island: families, groups of friends, happy couples. And when Kook parents leave their kids, it's to go on business trips in suits and ties with first-class tickets in their pockets and itineraries in their calendars. Their fathers don't disappear on them the way mine disappeared on me. Maybe that's the biggest difference between the Kooks and the Pogues—not the money, or the attitudes, or the mansions, or the yachts, but the kind of parents that Kooks have.

Not that I wish my dad were someone else. He's my *dad*. I just wish he could have been the sort of dad who didn't pull a disappearing act.

But there's something nobody knows. Not my friends, not Uncle Teddy, definitely not the authorities who wanted me to say Dad was gone for good. A week before he left the last time, Dad told me he might need to vanish for a bit. He didn't say why, but it was clear: he didn't want me to think the worst if he was gone for a while. Maybe the whole reason Dad raised me on stories of sailors who made their way home after so much time was to make sure I wouldn't give up hope when he disappeared one day.

So, I won't.

✳ ✳ ✳

I don't remember falling asleep last night, but I must've crashed on the couch because I wake to the sound of JJ shouting my name as he walks inside. I open my eyes just enough to see him opening the screen door and stepping over a pile of dirty laundry, then around a pyramid we built from empty beer and soda cans. He knocks over a box of cereal, sending Cheerios everywhere. Or anyway, they would go everywhere if there wasn't another pile of laundry blocking their path.

Like homework, housekeeping hasn't exactly been high on my priority list since Dad left.

"Hey, John B." JJ's voice drops to a whisper. "You up?"

I resist the urge to point out how obvious it is that I am *not* up, he's literally face-to-face with my half-asleep body. I open my eyes and pull myself to sit. I'm still wearing the jeans I had on last night, the black shirt I wore to sneak across the golf course. JJ left the door open when he came inside and there's a cool breeze coming off the water. The house may not resemble the mansions I passed last night, but just like them, it's on the water. Our boat—the HMS *Pogue*—is tied to the dock out back.

"I'm up," I say finally, swinging my legs over the side of the couch. I pull out my phone and squint. "JJ, what are you doing here? It's seven in the morning." We didn't get home from the beach until well after midnight last night.

"Couldn't sleep much," JJ answers with a shrug. He sits down on the coffee table in front of me, crushing the empty pizza box, then gets up. He paces

39

across the room, stepping on the mess like it's not even there. JJ gets jittery from time to time, but I've never seen him quite like this.

"Dude, did you, like, shotgun twenty Red Bulls or something?"

"What?" JJ asks, looking distracted. "No. Just, like I said, couldn't sleep."

"Okay," I say slowly. I reach toward the coffee table and shake one lukewarm soda can after another, trying to find the one that's least empty to take a drink from. The Coke is flat and stale.

JJ spins to face me. "So, I've been thinking."

"Really?" I ask. "How can you tell?"

JJ rolls his eyes. "Shut up. Listen, it's bullshit that only the Kooks get to take off for spring break."

"What do you mean? We take off. I mean, we're off school."

"I'm not talking about school." JJ starts pacing again. "I mean, that they actually *go* somewhere, stay at a fancy hotel, that kind of thing."

"Well, screw it," I say. "Life's not fair, isn't that what grown-ups are always telling us?"

"I'm not talking about *fair*," JJ spits. "I'm talking about *fun*."

"What kind of fun?" I ask warily. I'm not exactly the most careful person in the world, but sometimes JJ's plans are too out there even for me.

"Well, I figure, if the Tourons *come* to our island for spring break, we should *leave*."

"And go where?" I ask. "Sneak into their empty mansions on the mainland?"

JJ grins. "Not a bad idea, but not what I had in mind." Finally, he sits,

40

perching on the edge of the coffee table in front of me. "How about a fishing trip—you and me and Pope and Kie?"

"A fishing trip? Dude, we've been over this. Spring break is the worst time for fishing in the OBX." The Tourons clear out the bait and tackle shops and crowd the marshes. You're more likely to catch their litter than an actual fish.

"I'm not talking about fishing in the OBX." JJ's eyes are wide with excitement. "I've got it all mapped out. We'll head to Frying Pan Shoals."

"The Graveyard of the Atlantic?"

"Huh?"

"That's what my dad called it." I smile, remembering. "Frying Pan Shoals is called the Graveyard of the Atlantic because of how many ships went down there over the years. It's like a mini–Bermuda Triangle. I mean, I think technically it's *in* the Bermuda Triangle." I feel myself gazing toward my dad's (locked) office door, knowing that he has every kind of nautical map in the world inside. He taught me about the shoals years ago.

"Anyway," I continue, "there's nothing there but a decommissioned light tower." Dad took me to see it once. "I think it was a bed-and-breakfast for a while, but that was, like, a couple of decades ago or something."

JJ shakes his head. "Dude, I'm not suggesting a romantic getaway to a B&B with you."

I raise my eyebrows, pretending to be offended. "Oh, you think you can do better than me?"

41

"*So* much better." JJ laughs. "But don't change the subject. We'd just go for a day or two. We'd sleep on the *Pogue*. We'll spearfish so we won't even need bait."

I rub my eyes. "So what you're suggesting is a guys' fishing trip to the Graveyard of the Atlantic on my boat."

"Yeah. Well, except for the guys part. 'Cause of Kie."

I hesitate. It's tempting. But I haven't spent a night away from this house since Dad disappeared.

What if he comes back and I'm not here?

JJ starts pacing again. "I mean, come on, man, how can you stand it?"

"Stand what?"

"Being trapped on this island when it's overrun with Kook Tourons like this. They take up all the space. They breathe all the air." He turns and looks at me meaningfully. "It's not like we both couldn't use a distraction from"— he pauses, looking around my empty, adult-less house—"from all this." JJ seems uncharacteristically somber for a second, and I think he's going to say something about his dad, or maybe my dad, but instead he says, "Screw the Kooks, right?"

He runs his hand through his blond hair, and I see the shadow of a fresh bruise on the left side of his face, somehow making his blue eyes look even brighter. I don't have to ask how he got it. And I'm definitely not about to ask if JJ wants to get out of town not just to avoid the Tourons, but to avoid his dad, too.

I look around my mess of a living room. I've lived here my whole life, but the truth is, I never feel more at home than when I'm on the water. I picture myself directing the *Pogue* through the marshes and out onto the ocean toward the shoals, standing with a speargun in my hand, searching for fish in the glassy shallows. I feel almost literally tugged toward the water.

Plus, JJ's right. It would be nice to get away from all the rich jerks crowding our island.

"Yeah," I agree finally. "Screw the Kooks."

CHAPTER 6

JJ

I HAVE NO CLUE WHAT TIME IT WAS WHEN I CAME UP WITH my Frying Pan Shoals fishing trip plan. Two, three, four in the morning?

I slept on and off all night. The hammock isn't exactly as comfortable as that plush bed over at the hotel. I spun my lighter in between my fingers, lighting it and then letting it go dark, lighting it and letting it go dark, for what felt like hours. I was too hot, and then I was too cold, and then the sun was coming up and it was too bright.

So I came over here, to John B's.

John B's place isn't actually that much more of a dump than mine, considering there aren't any grown-ups around to tell him to pick up after himself. I mean, my dad doesn't exactly keep things clean, but he does occasionally growl, "Clean up this mess," before he passes out. Sometimes I do. Clean up, I mean.

Most times I don't. It's not my job to clean up my father's messes.

Now, John B asks, "Won't your dad be pissed if you just take off for a couple of days?"

I shrug. Dad probably didn't notice that I never came inside last night, and he won't notice that I'm gone today. I don't think he thinks about me at all, unless I'm standing right in front of him.

And then, it's not like the thoughts are good.

Anyway, this isn't just about me. It's about John B. It's not good for him to sit around his house every day, waiting for his dad to come home.

Sometimes I think the wrong dad went missing.

A lot of the time, actually.

But that's the sort of thing you think and don't ever say out loud. Even me, and I never think before I speak. At least, that's what Kiara says—that I should think before I say stuff.

Plus, I don't really mean it. Even if Big John has always been the better dad. But it's still a horrible thing to think. Like, what if just thinking it is enough to, I don't know, send bad luck my dad's way or something? Not that I believe in magic or curses or that kind of thing.

But still.

"Come on, man," I say to John B now. "Let's get some supplies."

We head to Heyward's to gather the sort of supplies we can buy in front of Pope's dad: bottles of water, boxes of cereal, and bags of chips. (As usual, the Tourons have cleared out the shelves and it's slim pickings, but we manage.) We'll have to get beer elsewhere. Maybe Kie can swipe some booze from the bar at The Wreck. If only the bottles in my shorts had survived last night's adventure.

We start loading supplies onto the *Pogue*, secured to the dock behind John B's place. We're not just bringing fishing poles and bait, but also heavy spearguns.

"Frying Pan Shoals is supposed to be some kind of spearfishing heaven," I say.

I read about it on my phone last night when I wasn't sleeping.

"Heaven sounds good," John B says, but he gazes out at the water, and suddenly I worry I've said something wrong. Like, if heaven is out on the water, and heaven is where we go when we die—if we're good and all that BS—then does John B think that's where his dad is, out there on the water somewhere?

I mean, I know John B doesn't believe his dad is dead. Or anyway, he *says* that he doesn't. But Big John's been gone awhile now. It's hard not to wonder if he might be, you know, not okay.

And I think, deep down, John B thinks about that, too.

Sometimes, at least.

All the more reason for us to get out on the water. Get out of the house, get John B's mind to focus on fish instead of fathers. Besides, maybe when we get back, his dad will be in the house, waiting.

You never know.

"What's on the radar?" John B asks.

"Huh?"

"The weather." John B rolls his eyes. "How're the conditions gonna be out there?" He nods at the water.

"Oh man, perfect. Ideal for fishing."

John B knows me well, but even he can't tell when I'm lying.

The truth is, until John B mentioned it, it hadn't occurred to me to check the weather. All I know is I need off this island, come rain or come shine.

Anyway, what do weathermen know? It's not like the guy on channel two was going to make a special report about conditions on the shoals if only I'd tuned in to watch. The weather on the water is tough to predict—they could've predicted a squall and we'd end up with sunshine or vice versa. I'm not about to let the possibility of bad weather keep us on dry land.

Conditions are perfect *now*. The sun is shining, there's a cool breeze off the water, not a cloud in the sky. It's not as warm as yesterday, so I'm wearing long pants and a sweatshirt with a vest over it, boots with thick socks, plus I brought a hat and gloves. It gets cold on the water.

"Come on, man," I say, jumping off the boat and onto the dock. "Let's round up the troops and hit the road. Or you know, hit the water."

John B grins, but then he shifts his gaze back out over the water. I don't think he knows how often he does that—stares out at the water like he's waiting for something. Which, you know, I guess he is. Well, not some-*thing*. Someone.

When he does that, it's like he can't hear me, or Kie, or Pope. It's like he's in a trance.

Maybe he's, like, praying, or something, to the sea gods to bring his dad home.

As we set off to find Kiara and Pope, I let John B take the lead. This time, I'm the one gazing back at the water. I say a silent prayer to the sea gods myself for good weather and a massive grouper with my name on it.

CHAPTER 7

JJ

"EXTRA CREDIT?" I SAY, LIKE THEY'RE TWO WORDS I'VE NEVER heard before.

I mean, of course I've heard them before, but I've sure as shit never *said* them before.

John B and I are standing in Pope's house. Pope's sitting at the kitchen table, a stack of books in front of him, a notebook covered in his neat handwriting—I swear, it looks like typing—under his palms. I grab it.

"Seriously, dude, you do realize we're on spring break, right?"

"Give it back, JJ," Pope says, reaching for the book. He looks worried that I'm going to, I don't know, rip up the pages into such tiny pieces that he'll spend spring break taping them back together instead of actually doing whatever extra credit project he's working on.

Pope is the kind of person who not only *does* extra credit but *asks* for it.

Like, I bet he went up to our science teacher after class on the last day of school and asked if he could have an assignment to work on over spring break.

Unlike my house or John B's, Pope's place is spotless. It's not any bigger than mine—just two bedrooms, one bathroom, all on one floor—but it looks about a million times nicer.

Pope has the kind of parents who gave him chores from the time he was a little kid. Like, literally there was a list of chores on the fridge door, and Pope made a check mark every time he got something done: made the bed, cleared the table, unloaded the dishwasher. Sometimes his mom would put a star or a plus sign next to the check when she thought Pope did a particularly good job.

Maybe that's when he started his love affair with good grades.

To tell you the truth, I think Pope is the kind of person who would keep things neat even if his parents didn't make him. Pope likes order and organization. Sometimes I catch him cleaning up the mess when we're all hanging out at John B's, like he literally can't have fun until he hauls the garbage out back or something.

Now, I hold his notebook up over my head, making moves like I'm going to tear the pages. I would never actually do that to Pope—I may think his devotion to school is ridiculous, but I know how much it means to him—but it's still a hell of a lot of fun to watch him squirm when I mess with him.

"Come on, man," Pope says, standing up so fast that he knocks his chair over. He looks pleadingly at John B, as though he thinks John B will be able to, I don't know, keep me in line or whatever.

But John B folds his arms across his chest and grins.

"I don't know, Pope. Homework sure does seem like a waste of spring break. Maybe"—he gets a twinkle in his eye, and I know he's about to mess with Pope, too—"maybe we should confiscate this notebook so you have no choice but to take this week off."

John B grabs the notebook from me and makes a show of pretending to consider what's written on the pages. "E=mc squared?" he starts. And then, " 'To be, or not to be'?" And then, "The quadratic equation?" None of these words are actually written on the notebook, but they're the sort of things teachers say.

John B holds it out of Pope's reach, parading around the living room.

"Come on, you guys," Pope pleads. "My dad'll kill me if I don't ace this project."

I roll my eyes. I mean, sure, Pope's dad would be disappointed, but Pope's even harder on himself about scoring straight A's.

John B turns to me. "What do you think, JJ, should we let this seasoned academic get back to work?" He pretends to have a British accent.

I shake my head. "You know, Pope, you're so obsessed with learning things. Maybe John B and I can teach you how to have a good time."

John B nods in agreement. "What a fine idea, JJ!" He continues in his fake-serious voice. "We should use this fishing trip to teach our friend here the value of a well-spent spring break."

"Seems to me that we'd be filling in a major gap in your education." In a deeper voice, I add, "To party, or not to party."

John B says, "To fish, or not to fish."

"To vacation, or to do homework."

Pope looks pained. John B and I grin, and John B tosses the notebook back to him.

"Consider this lesson number one," John B says, letting Pope off the hook.

"We'll continue our studies when we get back from the shoals," I add.

Pope looks so relieved when we walk out the door that I burst out laughing.

"I've never seen anyone so scared at the prospect of *not* doing their homework," I say.

John B shrugs. "Yeah, well, Pope is Pope."

"Pope is Pope," I echo.

✳ ✳ ✳

"Not you, too!" I exclaim. Now, I'm at The Wreck, and Kie won't stand still long enough to have an actual conversation. So I follow her around as she moves from one table to another, balancing a tray on her shoulder, providing tourists with drinks and fried clams and crab legs and whatever the hell else they want. She's wearing light blue jeans and a sweatshirt with "The Wreck" written across her chest. Her long hair is pulled into a bun balancing precariously on the top of her head.

Not for the first time, I wonder why she bothers spending time with John B, Pope, and me. She could literally hang with anyone she wants.

John B left me to get Kie on my own. He went back to finish getting the *Pogue* ready to head out to the shoals.

"Come on, JJ," Kie says in between taking orders and giving smiles so fake I'm surprised even the Kooks can't see through them, "I already told you my dad was making me work for spring break."

"Yeah, but that was before."

"Before what?"

"Before I came up with this excellent plan."

Kiara stops moving long enough to look me in the eye. "Remind me the plan again."

"A fishing trip to Frying Pan Shoals," I say for what seems like the hundredth time.

Kiara rolls her eyes. "JJ, I don't even *like* fishing. I get enough fish here, believe me."

"The fishing isn't the point!" I argue. "I mean, it is for John B and me, but you can just, I don't know, lie on the boat and soak up the sun."

"It's March, not August," Kie points out reasonably. "More like I'll be shivering while you guys compare fish size." Kiara gives me a good-natured shove, then brushes past me to pick up an order from the kitchen.

"Come on," I say. "You know as well as I do that John B needs this."

Finally, Kiara gives me her undivided attention, pulling me into a (relatively) quiet corner of the restaurant.

"What do you mean?" she asks in a low voice.

"Kie, we can't leave him sitting in that empty house for all of spring break, waiting for Big John to come home."

"If he ever comes home," Kie adds, biting her lip.

"Exactly," I agree.

I don't mention that *I* need this, too. That I can't spend spring break trapped in the house with my dad any more than John B can spend it trapped in his house without his dad. I hope Kie can't see the bruise on my face from Dad's latest slap.

I don't want Kie feeling sorry for me.

I don't want *anyone* feeling sorry for me.

Anyway, as much as I hate to admit it, I don't think feeling sorry for *me* would be enough to get Kie on the boat. But feeling sorry for John B might.

"You're right," Kie says, and just as I'm sure she's about to give in, her father calls her name from across the restaurant.

"Kiara!" he shouts. "Table two is waiting on their clam strips!"

Kiara's face shifts and I know she's not thinking about John B anymore. She's thinking about her dad and the restaurant and table two.

Crap.

So much for tugging at her heartstrings or whatever.

"I can't, JJ," Kiara says finally. "I wish I could. You know I would come if I could."

"Yeah." I try not to sound too disappointed because she really does sound sorry. "I know you would."

"Catch a big one for me," she says, and for a second I think she's going to, like, kiss my cheek or something.

"You hate fishing," I remind her. John B, Pope, and I have had to listen to lecture after lecture about how the overfishing of the oceans has contributed to the calamity of climate change.

"Yeah, I do," Kie agrees. "But you guys love it. So have fun."

"We will. Though not as much fun if you were there."

Kiara grins, then adds, "And take care of John B."

"I will," I promise.

In my pocket, I finger the Swiss Army knife I swiped from Dad this morning. Kie must know that *I* can take care of myself.

CHAPTER 8

JOHN B

I DIRECT THE *POGUE* THROUGH THE MARSHES BEHIND THE Chateau. She's just an old skiff—we've had her forever—but I know her like the back of my hand, so I'm (mostly) confident she can take us to the shoals and back.

JJ's come up with some ridiculous plans over the years, but I have to give him credit: This fishing trip is actually a good idea. Even though it's cool out, the sun is bright overhead, reflecting off the water.

"Kiara and Pope have no idea what they're missing," JJ says, taking a seat in the bow and propping his legs on the cooler. "Wait till we come back with a boatload of giant grouper."

I shake my head. Kie doesn't even like fishing—JJ was always going to have a hard time convincing her to join. And it's pretty much impossible to pry Pope away from his schoolwork. Still, I can't remember the last time it was just JJ and me like this.

I've never been to Frying Pan Shoals by myself, but I know exactly how to get there, thanks to my dad. He taught me that Frying Pan Shoals is a long, shifting area of shoals off Cape Fear River. And, FYI, shoals are sandbanks and sandbars that make the water shallow—they can take the place of a mound or a ridge of sand just below the water, which is why they're so dangerous. A boat can be sailing along, its captain believing he's in deep water, when all of a sudden it hits a shoal.

Frying Pan Shoals has been hazardous for ships and sailors going back to European exploration of the area, like back when the United States was just a handful of colonies. According to Dad, from 1994 to 2008, more than 130 shipwreck locations were discovered in the area. So . . . yeah, it's a dangerous place, even for experienced boatmen. But fish gather in and around shoals, which is why it's a great fishing destination. In warm weather, you can stand up to your knees in water on a shoal and spear a fish swimming along beside you.

JJ shakes his head in disgust as a shiny Kook/tourist speedboat rushes past us, splashing us with water.

"They'll let anybody rent a boat these days," JJ complains. You're not supposed to drive that fast here in the marshes, but clearly these Tourons don't care.

I direct the *Pogue* back and forth behind the other boat, so we're bouncing up and down in its wake, almost like our little boat is surfing. The *Pogue* may just be an old skiff, but I can show those tourists that I can do more with an old skiff than they can do with the newest, most expensive boat money can buy.

"Yeah!" JJ shouts approvingly.

Dad taught me how to drive a boat before I learned to drive a car. He took me fishing on Sundays the way other dads take their kids to church. He taught me to read nautical maps with the same intensity other people's dads apply to teaching their kids to learn letters and read words or to memorize their multiplication tables. I can't remember the first time he took me out on the water. I mean, literally, I *can't*, I was too young to even make the memory. I learned to swim before I learned to walk. At least, that's what Dad told me—like I said, I was too young to remember.

The *Pogue* bounces across the other boat's wake. Finally, I turn sharply and send a splash onto their boat the same way they did to us. The Tourons shout at us, but JJ shouts back, "You started it!"

I direct the *Pogue* out of the marshes toward the open ocean.

I can still remember the first Sunday morning when JJ just showed up at the Chateau. We were only six or seven. (I actually can't really remember a time before I knew JJ.) JJ's dad was hungover after one of his Saturday night benders. JJ had an almost-empty box of stale cereal in his hands when he showed up at our house at the crack of dawn. Kind of like how he showed up this morning. I guess not much has changed where that's concerned.

Anyway, that morning my dad made scrambled eggs for the three of us and loaded us onto the boat. JJ and I had to share a fishing pole. Dad told us that legend has it groupers never stop growing, right up until the day they die. Every time JJ and I looked down into the water we imagined we saw giants floating in the depths.

We didn't see any giant groupers, but we caught a couple of regular-sized ones and watched dolphins play in the waves on our way home. Dad taught us how to clean the fish and cooked them on the grill when we got home, and I swear, nothing I've eaten since that day has ever tasted so good.

After that, JJ showed up nearly every Sunday, as long as the weather was good and my dad wasn't off on one of his trips without me. I didn't mind that JJ came with us most of the time. But, now that my dad is gone, I kind of wish he and I had had more time to ourselves. Maybe, if it had been just the two of us, I'd have asked Dad more questions. Maybe if I'd asked the right questions, I'd know where he is right now. Maybe he'd never have left. Maybe he'd have taken me with him.

Eventually, Dad and I (and JJ) stopped fishing together on Sundays. As I got older, I started wanting to spend my weekends with my friends instead of with my dad. Which seems so stupid now.

I'll make up for it, when he gets back. We'll start spending Sundays together again. He'll fill my head with stories about where he's been just like he used to fill it with stories of giant groupers and nautical facts and phrases.

"Dude," JJ says, interrupting my thoughts. "You look like you're in outer space."

I shake my head. "I was just thinking about how we used to fish with my dad."

JJ sits in the captain's chair, propping his legs in front of him. "Man, those were good times. Your dad taught us everything we know about how to catch fish."

I nod. "Remember the first time he took us spearfishing?" We were twelve, and Dad left the fishing poles at home and took us into the marshes. We had only one speargun, so JJ and I took turns with it.

He made sure we understood just how dangerous it was, made us promise never to do it without him around to supervise.

I wonder if he'd be mad at us now, heading out to spearfish without him. Maybe he thinks we're old enough to supervise ourselves now.

After all, he left. He thought I was old enough for *that*. Though maybe he thought Uncle Teddy would be a better guardian than he turned out to be.

JJ says, "Remember how I speared my first fish before you did?"

"No way!" I counter. "I speared at least three before you even got one." I caught a fish on my second try. Dad clapped me on the back and whistled, like my skills had blown him away.

JJ pretends that he's thinking really hard. "That's not how I remember it."

I'm about to make a joke about JJ's faulty memory when I realize—if only my dad were here, he could tell us how he remembers that day, settle who caught the first fish. Suddenly, I miss my dad so much it aches. I kind of always miss him, but sometimes it's more acute.

"You know," JJ continues (he has no idea what's going on in my head at the moment), "your dad was the one who got me interested in how engines work."

60

"Really?"

"Yeah," JJ says. "Don't you remember? That time the *Pogue*'s engine kept flooding, and your dad and I practically had to take the whole boat apart and put her together again to get back home."

I shake my head. "I don't remember that at all." JJ's probably exaggerating. The engine just sort of hangs off the back of the boat. You'd hardly have to take the boat apart to get it working.

JJ cocks his head to the side, his blond hair flying around his face thanks to the ocean breezes. I'm wearing a baseball cap to keep my hair in check and to keep my gaze sharp when the sun glints off the water. "Oh, you know what, I don't think you were with us that time."

"I wasn't with you?" I echo.

"Yeah, I can't remember. It was—I think it was, like, a Wednesday or something and I was cutting school. You were too much of a goody two shoes to cut with me, so I showed up at your dad's and we headed out onto the water."

"Goody two shoes?" I feign offense.

"Well, not, like, Pope-level good, but better than me."

JJ grins, but I don't smile back. Suddenly, I feel, I don't know, like *jealous* or something that JJ spent time with my dad without me. I didn't get to spend nearly enough time with Dad. Even when I was younger, he was always leaving on one trip after another after another, in search of I have no idea what. I should've asked him where he was going, why he was going, what he was looking for. I think of all the Sundays that we could have spent fishing together, just the two of us, if only Dad stuck around—and if only I'd told JJ to stay home. And maybe, if it had just been the two of us, I'd have asked all those questions. But instead I was distracted, goofing off with JJ.

I shake myself like a puppy after a bath, reminding myself that JJ didn't do anything wrong. JJ's dad is the *worst*. Definitely not the kind of dad who'll patiently teach you to repair an engine or spearfish or really anything else. Maybe JJ needed that time with my dad as much as I did.

But I can't get rid of the feeling that I lost precious time.

"Did you ever think that maybe it was kind of weird that you spent so much time with someone else's parent?" My voice sounds somehow *harder* than usual. I try to control it, but I can't.

"Weird?" JJ echoes. "Your dad was awesome."

"*Was* awesome?" I hate the sound of anyone talking about my dad in the past tense, like he's never coming back.

JJ shakes his head frantically. "I didn't mean *was* like that! I meant, like, when we were kids is all."

Maybe this fishing trip wasn't a good idea. It's just another one of JJ's wild schemes, and we'd be better off turning back right now.

I should be at home anyway. Just in case.

The engine sputters and I lean over to check on it. We'll never get back home if the engine gives out. When I straighten, JJ is standing over me, a spear in his hand, a wild look on his face.

CHAPTER 9

JJ

"DUDE, WHAT ARE YOU DOING?" JOHN B SHOUTS.

"Don't you remember?" I ask. I'd never, you know, *hurt* John B—well, not on purpose. But I had to do something extreme to get his mind off his dad. The whole point of this trip is to distract him from worrying about his dad.

And to give me a break from mine.

"Remember what?" John B asks.

"Our first solo fishing trip!"

John B grins.

Almost as soon as Big John taught us to spearfish, I was hooked. And sure, he made us promise not to head out on the water without him, but I couldn't help myself.

"Let's hope this trip goes better than that one did," John B says.

"Oh, come on, it wasn't that bad."

"How much worse could it get than you literally spearing me in the foot?"

"It was just a scratch!" I insist.

"I nearly lost a toe!"

I roll my eyes, pretending to be exasperated. "Don't be so dramatic."

It was the summer after seventh grade and Big John wasn't around, something that was starting to happen more and more often. I mean, he'd always had mysterious trips, but it got so he almost never had time to take us fishing. He was never gone for more than a day or two back then, though. Guess he knew he couldn't leave John B alone then the way he did this time.

Anyway, I convinced John B it would be a good idea to grab his speargun—I didn't have one of my own back then—and wade into the marsh behind the Chateau. *Just for practice*, I promised. We wouldn't actually loose the spear. It was just to practice our technique for the next time Big John took us out. But when it was my turn to hold the spear, I got bored and started horsing around—playing like I was aiming for John B instead of the fish—and then I accidentally let the spear go.

"It was an accident," I say, lowering the spear.

John B shakes his head. "That didn't make it hurt any less," he points out, but he's smiling.

Big John got home late that night, and he took us to the hospital. John B got three spidery black stitches in his big toe. When my own dad finally showed up and asked what happened, Big John covered for me. He said he'd been there the whole time, the fishing trip was his idea. I'd never had anybody lie like that for me before.

But later, he took me aside and made me promise not to be so reckless.

"You and John B have to take care of each other," he said. He didn't seem mad, but I'd never seen Big John look so solemn. Now, I wonder if maybe he knew he wouldn't always be around to take care of John B . . . and it was obvious by then that my dad had already given up on taking care of me.

Sometimes I think John B and I take better care of each other than our dads ever did.

✳ ✳ ✳

As we approach the shoals, John B navigates the *Pogue* carefully. They don't call it the Graveyard of the Atlantic for nothing—one wrong turn and our little boat could get stuck on a sandbar.

But conditions are perfect. The water is smooth and glassy beneath us. I breathe a secret sigh of relief.

"What do you think, is this a good spot?" John B asks.

"Yeah." I nod approvingly. "I can practically feel the giant groupers about to gather." John B rolls his eyes but drops anchor.

It's not like I didn't know that I was intruding sometimes, with John B and Big John. I mean, John B and his dad never actually *said* anything about it—but once in a while I worried that maybe they didn't want me around. I didn't think of it as taking John B's dad away from him, though. I mean, if someone offered to take *my* dad's focus off me once in a while, I'd literally thank them for it.

But now I worry that maybe—if Big John doesn't come back—John B will actually look back on all those fishing trips like they're time I stole from him, time when it could have been just the two of them that I took away just be being there.

Okay, now I'm the one who needs a distraction.

Luckily, spearfishing takes total concentration. It's not like dropping a line in the water and waiting for something to take a bite. Big John taught me that. He said that spearfishing has been around for thousands of years. I remember once he told me—he was holding his hands over mine on a speargun, teaching me how to use it—that somewhere in France there are cave paintings that are over sixteen thousand years old that include drawings of seals that have been harpooned.

These days, some spear-fishers actually scuba dive into deep waters with their spearguns. It's illegal in some places, since some species of fish were hunted until they became endangered. (Cue one of Kiara's speeches.)

The best kind of water for spearfishing is calm and shallow and clear. Big John told us that the kind of spearfishing we're doing—from our boat in shallow waters—is the most ancient kind, though we're using a speargun, which they definitely didn't have thousands of years ago.

There are two types of spearguns: pneumatic and elastic. (Ours are elastic.) The gun launches a tethered spear or harpoon to impale the fish. The handle has a trigger that you use to shoot the spear, so it's sort of halfway between taking aim with a rifle and using a bow and arrow.

John B and I stare over the side of the boat into the water, waiting for a fish to make an appearance.

After a few minutes of staring in silence, I say, "I guess Kie has a point."

"About what?"

"She says fishing is boring." I mean, I love the actual catching of the fish part, but the watching and waiting part definitely isn't my favorite.

John B shakes his head. "This isn't boring. It's exciting, waiting for a fish to show up."

"You sound like Pope, the way he gets excited about studying. Like *learning* something new is as much fun as actually *doing* something new."

John B shrugs. "For Pope, I guess it is."

"I guess so," I agree absently, but I definitely don't understand it.

Suddenly, John B points. Below us is what looks like a grouper. Not exactly a giant, but still, it's pretty big. John B holds up his speargun, silently asking if he can shoot first. I nod. He lets his spear loose into the water. I ready myself behind him, to give him extra support if he needs it. It's not unheard of for someone to get pulled off a boat and into the water. A lot of spear-fishermen fish while standing in the actual water, but it's too cold for that today without wetsuits.

John B misses.

"Too high," I say, and John B nods in agreement. When you see a fish, you have to consider the way the light on the water can make the fish look higher than it really is and aim lower than it seems like you need to.

John B pulls his line out of the water, locking his spear back into place. I look back down, but the fish he was aiming for is gone. I move to the starboard side of the boat and look down. And I swear, I see the biggest fish I've ever seen.

Without pausing to get John B's attention, I take aim. From there, it all happens fast.

I feel the tip of my spear hit something.

Something *huge*.

Something that wants to get away.

I keep my grip tight.

And then I'm in the water.

Icy water fills my nose, my ears, my mouth. I sputter to the surface. I can hear John B calling my name. I've never been so cold in my life. Normally, you'd wear a head-to-toe wetsuit in water this cold.

"Let go," John B shouts, but I get pulled under again. I can't hear John B's voice anymore. The fish is swimming away from the boat and dragging me after him.

I manage to make it to the surface again and take a breath before the fish pulls me under.

When Big John taught us to spearfish, he made sure we understood that it was dangerous. He had us promise never to do it without him. He told us stories about fishermen who'd been drowned by their prey, about boatloads of whalers who'd drowned in what they called the Nantucket sleighride. (Cue another speech from Kiara about the inhumanity of the whaling industry.) Big John thought all those stories would scare us.

And I don't know, maybe they scared John B.

But they didn't scare me. They *excited* me.

Suddenly the rope of my speargun goes slack. I paddle to the surface, blinking salt water out of my eyes and spinning around until I see the *Pogue*. John B is practically hanging over the side. I can see that his mouth is moving—he must still be shouting my name—but I can't hear him from this far away. I start swimming, grateful that I took my phone out of my pocket and placed it on the bench in the back of the *Pogue* before we dropped anchor. It would've been ruined otherwise.

"What were you thinking?" John B asks when I'm finally back in ear-shot. He pulls me over the side of the boat. I'm shivering and my teeth are chattering. John B wraps towel after towel around me, rubbing my shoulders. "How could you loose your spear without telling me? I would've had your back, man."

He's right—if I'd let him know before I took my shot, John B would've stood behind me. He could've used his body weight to help keep me on the boat. Salt water drips off the ends of my hair and into my eyes. John B grabs the speargun out of my hand—somehow, I'm still holding it—and I see that my fingers are bright red from squeezing so tight. The muscles in my hand are spasming, making my whole arm shake.

John B retracts the spear into the gun. On the tip of the spear is a chunk of . . . something.

"That monster fish literally ripped himself off the tip of the spear," I say.

"Guess he didn't want to die today," John B says. His voice hardens as he adds, "Unlike you. You're lucky you didn't get hypothermia, let alone drown."

"What do you mean?" I ask. "I wasn't, like, trying to drown."

"Well, then why didn't you drop the speargun?"

"It's the only one I have!" I explain. "What, would we have just taken turns using yours all day?" Plus—and I won't say this part out loud—my dad would kill me if I lost it.

"We shared when we were kids," John B reminds me. I grit my teeth to stop their chattering.

John B shakes his head as he rips the chunk of fish off my spear and tosses it into the water.

"You know, JJ, one of these days, one of your ideas might be wild enough that you get yourself killed."

I shake my head. "Not yet," I counter. "I'm still here, aren't I?"

"Whatever," John B says.

"Come on," I tease. I'm starting to warm up. "Think how much less exciting this expedition of ours would be if I hadn't just gotten dragged into the ocean by a two-ton grouper."

"Two tons?" John B echoes. "More like two pounds, you lightweight."

"No way, that was the biggest fish I've ever seen! One of those giant groupers, no question."

John B ignores me. "Wait till I tell Kie and Pope how a teensy-weensy fish pulled you overboard."

"Wait till I tell them about how you couldn't even hit anything."

We keep going back and forth like that for a few minutes, until I'm sure John B's not pissed anymore.

The truth is: It didn't occur to me to drop the speargun, just like it didn't occur to me not to shoot at that giant fish. It would've been easy, if I let go of the spear, to swim over to some shallow spot and stand up. The only way I would've drowned is if the fish pulled me under, and the only reason he could pull me under is because I didn't let go of the gun.

Kie's always saying I should think before I speak.

If she were here right now, she'd say I should think before I act, too.

I wasn't trying to get myself killed. I wasn't trying to make trouble—really. I saw the fish and so I let the spear go.

It's the sort of thing Kie, and Pope, and even John B, would never do.

Anyway, I always seem to get into trouble. It doesn't matter what I'm *trying* to do.

CHAPTER 10

JOHN B

HOLY SHIT, MAN. MY HEART IS STILL POUNDING. WHEN JJ went overboard, my brain started automatically making a mental list of the ways that he could die:

1. Drowning. Despite the shallow water, the fish might have held him under. You can drown in three inches of water, after all. People drown at home in their own bathtubs.

2. Hypothermia. You're really not supposed to be in water this cold without a wetsuit, and even then you're at risk.

3. A shark attack. The blood from the grouper might attract a predator.

From there, my brain just kept going, expanding the list into all the ways people can die on the water: getting caught in a storm, falling overboard, having their boat malfunction in some way that traps them until they run out of food and potable water without a chance of rescue.

As much as I love the ocean, I know how dangerous it can be. My dad made sure I had a healthy respect for the risks before he let me take the helm of our boat, before he taught me to fish or surf.

No one knows how dangerous it can be more than the people who actually spend a lot of time on the water.

People like my dad.

Usually, knowing that my dad is knowledgeable and careful comforts me. I can tell myself that it's the careless people who get hurt, go missing, fall overboard, and drown. Like JJ, carelessly spearing that fish.

But the truth is, even careful people can get hurt out here.

✳ ✳ ✳

Once JJ is safely back on the boat we shift our focus back to the water. I keep my gaze trained on the shallows, looking for a flicker of movement. After all this, we damn well better catch a fish or two.

"Remember how your dad used to say that fishing was the closest he came to meditation and all that new age crap?" JJ asks.

"Yeah," I say, though I feel myself bristle at the way JJ asks the question, like he thinks *he* might remember something about my dad that I don't. Of *course* I remember what Dad used to say about fishing.

"Keeping still, staring at the water, waiting for a sign of life. I remember he said that sometimes a whole hour had passed before he realized it. Never when we were around, though."

"Not exactly possible to achieve nirvana when you won't shut up," I say. JJ grins. He never keeps still or quiet for very long. But the truth is, it wasn't just JJ. Put the two of us together and we're always up to something, especially when we were little.

But sometimes, when it was just me and my dad, I'd be like him: holding my focus on the water alone, waiting for a fish to make an appearance, getting so used to the feel of the spear in my hand that it was like the speargun was an extension of my arm. I never made it a whole hour without noticing, but sometimes I'd go ten, twenty, once even thirty minutes, just sitting perfectly still like my dad.

"What the hell is that?" JJ shouts, breaking my concentration. It's not really possible to Zen out when JJ is around. He's whatever the opposite of meditation is.

I look up. There's a boat heading toward us. It's bigger than the *Pogue* and so clean and new that the sun reflects off the hull, making the water around it dazzle. "Looks like a Grady-White," I mumble, and JJ nods. Grady-White is a way expensive boat brand.

The bright, shiny boat moves slowly and carefully through the shoals. At least whoever's at the wheel isn't stupid enough to speed through the Graveyard of the Atlantic.

As the boat gets closer, I can see a girl standing at the bow, drink in hand and wearing rubber boots. She's practically balancing over the front edge of the boat, like one of those mermaid figureheads that used to be at the front of pirates' ships.

"That girl's gonna get herself killed," JJ says. I can't tell whether he's exasperated or impressed.

The boat keeps coming closer. It's bigger—and nicer—than I realized at first. Looks like it's barely spent any time outside of a marina. Then they drop anchor within shouting distance. JJ and I exchange a look.

"Hey," JJ calls out. "You've got the whole ocean! What are you doing parking right next to us?"

The girl chuckles, tossing her long hair over her shoulder, then pulling it into a bun just as efficiently as Kiara does. (Are girls born knowing how to do that sort of thing?) "We heard this was the place for spearfishing," she calls back.

JJ turns to me and says in a low voice, "Please. Like *they* know how to spearfish."

I shrug. I know it'd be pointless to suggest we wait to pass judgment until we've seen them in action.

But JJ might be right. Behind the girl are a handful of Kooks—I'm assuming they're Kooks, no one else could afford a boat that nice—who look more interested in getting wasted than in catching an actual fish. Some guy puts his arms around the girl from behind, kissing her neck so that she squeals in surprise and follows him below deck.

"Oh, shit," JJ says.

"What?"

"Those two—I think that's the couple from last night."

"Which couple?"

"Which couple?" JJ echoes incredulously. "The one whose room we got caught in. The girl who chased us through the hotel and tried to have us, I don't know, arrested or whatever."

"Savannah." Now I remember Kiara saying her name. But seriously, what are the odds that it's the same girl? "Dude, I know you think she's hot, but are you seriously hallucinating that she followed you out to the middle of the Atlantic Ocean now? Maybe you've had enough sun for one day."

I hold out my hand like I'm checking his forehead for a fever the way moms on TV do. JJ shrugs off my touch.

"I never said she was hot. And *you're* the one who remembers her name," JJ argues. "Anyway, I'm telling you, man, that's her. Same brown hair. Same long legs—"

"I didn't realize you got such a close look while she was running after us," I retort, but the truth is, I noticed her, too. "Come on," I say reasonably. "We're miles from home. The girl from the hotel is probably getting a massage or something in the resort spa while her jerky boyfriend plays a round of golf."

But then the girl and the guy emerge onto the deck of their boat with beer cans in hand and I have to admit JJ's right—it's definitely the same couple.

"Maybe she doesn't remember us?" I suggest hopefully.

"Oh yeah," JJ answers sarcastically. "It's not like anything we did last night was particularly memorable."

Remembering the way JJ lost his shorts, I laugh so hard I snort. JJ shoves me.

"Shut up," he says.

"You shut up," I answer, smacking him back.

The girl holds her hand up over her eyes like a visor. It's cool but sunny, the light reflecting off the glassy water beneath us.

"Hey," she shouts. "I recognize you two. You're the jerks who snuck into our room last night."

JJ laughs confidently. "Come on," he says. "We're in the middle of the ocean. What are the odds that we're the same two guys who stole your Mo-et a day ago?"

"It's pronounced *Mo-ay*," the girl corrects. "And you owe my boyfriend a hundred dollars."

"A hundred bucks for that bottle of piss?" JJ asks incredulously.

"In fact," Savannah continues, "now that I know what your boat looks like, when we get back tonight, I'm calling the authorities."

I hold up my hands. "There's no need for that," I say calmly, but the girl starts taking pictures with her shiny new iPhone like she's a cop taking mug shots.

JJ adds, "Why don't you and that pretty boy—"

"Hunter," Savannah provides smoothly. "And thanks, I think he's pretty, too."

"I didn't mean it as a compliment!" JJ insists, but Savannah smiles.

"Anyway," I break in. "Like JJ said, there's a whole ocean out here. No need for us to anchor side by side."

Savannah shrugs. "So why don't you move?"

JJ growls, "Why don't you and your friends leave the fishing to people who actually know what they're doing?"

Savannah lowers her phone and puts her hands on her hips. "What makes you think we don't know what we're doing?"

"Your friends look a lot more interested in getting wasted than bagging fish," I say. Savannah glances back at her friends, drinking beer on the deck behind her. One of them turns on some terrible music. It's obvious they're hardly even interested in this conversation, let alone in fishing.

JJ adds, "No one in a boat that shiny and new has any real experience on the water."

"It's a rental," Savannah explains with a shrug.

This is the most I've ever seen JJ talk to a Kook, and that's counting the Touron Kooks he hooked up with last summer. I work for the Camerons, so I *have* to talk to Kooks from time to time.

I turn to JJ and say, "Look, man, it's not like we've had any luck here since my miss and your near-death experience. Why don't we move on?"

JJ looks at me like I've just suggested that he cut off his own arm. "No way. I'm not leaving to make space for a bunch of Kooks."

"Well, we can't make them leave," I point out reasonably. "And I don't want to piss that girl off. She looks like she might seriously turn us in to the cops." DCS—the Department of Child Services—has already been sneaking around my house too much, between my unreliable Uncle Teddy and my MIA dad. The words *foster care* have been mentioned too many times already. If I got into some kind of legal trouble, they'd skip right over threatening me with foster care and send me straight to juvenile hall, or wherever they send kids these days.

"For stealing a bottle of shitty wine?"

"And for breaking into her room—"

"We didn't break in," JJ protests. "She left the door unlocked."

"Okay, but it's definitely still trespassing or whatever."

JJ looks pained. The last thing he wants to do is give in to a Touron.

"Come on," I add. "Kie and Pope could get into trouble, too."

Savannah breaks into our conversation, shouting, "Of course, I'd be happy to make a deal."

JJ turns back to her. "What kind of deal?" he asks warily.

"If you bag more fish than we do, I won't turn you in."

"There are two of us and, like, five of you!" JJ shouts.

"Six!" Savannah corrects cheerfully. "But if we don't know anything about spearfishing, what are you worried about anyway?"

"Okay, but what if you bag more fish?" I ask.

Savannah cocks her head to the side like she's trying to think about what JJ and I could possibly have that she might want.

"Then you owe Hunter for the champagne," she says reasonably. "And you have to get out of here and let us fish in peace."

"You're on," JJ says.

"Hey," I whisper. "We don't have that kind of money."

JJ nudges me. "You really think we have to worry that these idiots might outfish us?"

I grin. "Okay," I agree. "Game on."

CHAPTER 11

JJ

WHAT THE HELL ARE A BUNCH OF TOURON KOOKS DOING fishing out here?

Bad enough they took over the island for spring break—now they've gotta take the whole ocean, too?

I mean, I know Frying Pan Shoals isn't the entire ocean, but we came out here to get *away* from the Kooks. And now they're blaring their shitty Kook music and drinking their fancy Kook beer and eating, I don't know, escargot or green juice or whatever the hell Kooks eat.

John B didn't believe me at first, but I knew it was her—the girl from the hotel. I'm not, you know, all mushy-gushy over girls, but let's just say that *she's* the kind of girl I'd remember.

And not just because she's pretty—which look, I'm not blind. However annoying she is and however *not* interested I am, I can also see that she's good-looking, or whatever, especially now that she's in jeans and a sweat-shirt instead of a boring dress and heels. But anyway, the reason I remembered her is because I never would've thought a Kook girl would chase a

81

bunch of Pogues through a fancy hotel over one bottle of wine, not matter how expensive it is.

Or, excuse me, *Mo-ay* champagne.

So I remembered her, but I don't care if I never see her again. In fact, I would have been happier if I *hadn't* seen her again, because then John B and I would still be out here all alone.

At least they won't be here for long. That was the easiest bet I ever took. John B and I aren't about to get outfished by a bunch of mainland Kooks, that much I know for sure. They're obviously not here to fish—they're here to party.

Though, I have to admit, it's a long way to travel to party on their rental boat—they could've dropped anchor hours closer to their hotel. And Savannah actually looks like she knows what she's doing.

I mean, *only* Savannah.

The two other Kook girls on board aren't even bothering to pick up their bright, shiny (probably also rented) spearguns. I squint. Actually, other than Savannah, only Hunter picks up his speargun. I can't hear what they're saying over their awful music, but it looks like Savannah is trying to tell Hunter exactly how spearfishing works. He seems to be listening attentively.

"Come on," John B urges, and I follow him to the starboard side of the *Pogue,* as far from the Tourons as we can get.

Still, I glance back and see Savannah and Hunter disappear into their boat and emerge wearing wetsuits. (They probably rented those, too.)

Savannah climbs over the edge of the boat and swims until she reaches a sandbar where, standing up, she's about waist-deep in the water. She holds her speargun overhead expertly, and she doesn't squeal or complain about how cold the water is.

Hunter follows her, holding his speargun overhead like he's worried about getting it wet.

Pathetic.

Finally, I turn away. John B and I stand with spearguns in hand, gazing down into the water, waiting for another giant to make an appearance.

"Just give me a heads-up before you let loose," John B says, "so I can keep you on the boat this time."

I nod absently, without taking my eyes off the water. I don't know how long we stand there silently before I hear a splash. John B and I both turn around—Hunter has loosed his spear into the water.

"I hit something!" he shouts.

I roll my eyes. "That's kind of the point," I mutter, and John B snickers.

Hunter struggles like whatever he hit, it's bigger and stronger than he is, and it doesn't want to die today.

Maybe my giant grouper came back for more.

"Is that what I looked like?" I ask John B.

"Nah," he says. "You didn't look nearly so surprised that you actually hit something. More pissed that whatever it was, it was bigger than you."

"Are you calling me small?" I scoff, pretending to be offended.

"Smaller than a giant grouper," John B replies.

"Thought you didn't think it was a giant," I tease, and John B shrugs. "He's gonna let go," I add as I watch Hunter struggle.

"For sure," John B agrees.

What happens next unfolds so fast that I'm not sure I really see it. Savannah grabs Hunter's spear. She's about half Hunter's size, but I guess she thinks she's stronger. Still, she doesn't get dragged into the water like I did.

But then she sort of—I don't know—dives after whatever it is that's on the other end of the spear, letting it drag her off the sandbar and into deeper waters.

"What the hell is that girl doing?" I shout to no one in particular.

"She's even crazier than you are," John B says.

"Yeah," I agree breathlessly.

"Let go!" Hunter shouts.

After a second, John B and I start shouting the same thing.

Savannah doesn't let go.

Whatever it is, it drags her farther and farther away from the boats.

John B tosses me a look and I nod. There's only one thing to do. He pulls up the anchor and I turn on the engine. We're following Savannah as closely as we can. I glance back at Hunter, who's still standing on the sandbar, looking dumbfounded. I'm not sure it occurred to him to go after her.

"Take the wheel," I say, and John B takes my place. "Stop!" I shout, and I dive into the water as John B cuts the engine. We don't argue about which one of us is going to jump.

John B would never actually say it out loud, but we both know I'm the stronger swimmer.

CHAPTER 12

JJ

SOMEHOW, THE WATER IS LESS COLD NOW THAN IT WAS WHEN I went overboard before. Maybe it's because this time, I jumped in willingly. Or maybe it's because adrenaline is coursing through my body, hot and tingly, as I swim out to Savannah.

I put my arms around her, feeling her slick wetsuit beneath my skin. Whatever is on the tip of her spear—Hunter's spear—it's a hell of a lot bigger and stronger than we are. We can't pull it in. All I can do is get her to let go.

"What are you doing?" she sputters as I lace my fingers through hers, wrapped tightly around Hunter's speargun. Savannah holds fast, and I have to concentrate to loosen one finger after another, all while treading water, getting pulled along with her. When she goes under, I feel myself letting go—it's an instinct, I can't help it—but then she's surfaces, and I grab her again.

Finally, I loosen her hold enough that the speargun goes flying away from us.

"What the hell?" Savannah shouts. "That was my fish!"

"Thank you would do just fine," I say, but Savannah is pissed.

"That's a dirty trick," she insists as she treads water. "Literally ripping my speargun away from me to keep me from winning the bet!"

"Who cares about the bet?" I shout back. "You could have gotten yourself killed! It's just a fish, not a death wish."

Okay, so maybe John B said almost the same thing to me earlier, but that was different.

This Touron Kook and her friends are nothing like John B and me.

Savannah shakes her head like there's no doubt in her mind that if I'd only left her alone, she'd have defeated the fish and hauled in an enormous catch, winning the bet and besting John B and me.

She starts swimming toward the *Pogue*—since we followed her, it's much closer than Savannah's Kook rental boat. Her arms slice through the water smoothly. I follow, but even though I'm a better than average swimmer, I'm not nearly as graceful or fast as she is. Plus, she has the advantage of a wetsuit.

She gets back to the *Pogue* before I do; John B reaches out a hand to help her on and then pulls me up afterward. Without asking, Savannah helps herself to one of the drinks in our cooler and sits down.

"I'm Savannah Rivera," she says, propping her feet up on the bow of the boat.

John B holds out a towel but Savannah shakes her head. "John B," he says, gesturing to himself, and then, pointing to me, "JJ." He doesn't say *JJ*

Maybank, or introduce himself as *John Booker Rutledge*. But I guess Kooks are more formal about these things.

"Take the towel," I say as I wrap myself up, shivering. "Your lips are practically turning blue."

"I'm fine," she says tightly. She's trying to hide it, but I can tell her teeth are chattering, even with the advantage of the wetsuit. I grab the towel from John B's hand and toss it at her. Reluctantly, she wraps it around her shoulders.

"I didn't need your help," she says, glaring at me. "I didn't need a knight in shining armor to jump in the water and rescue me. I'm a good swimmer."

"Not as good as that fish," John B quips, and finally Savannah laughs, her hardened expression turning into a smile. She balances her drink between her legs and reaches up to squeeze some of the salt water out of her hair.

"A knight in shining armor would have drowned," I point out, trying for a joke like John B, but John B and Savannah look at me like I'm talking nonsense. "You know, because his armor would have weighed him down in the water?"

Savannah rolls her eyes. "It was a *metaphor.*"

She sighs heavily, like she thinks I'm the stupidest person she's ever met.

"It doesn't matter how good of a swimmer you are," I say testily. "You still could have gotten hurt, or worse. And not that you seem to care, but I could've gotten hurt, too."

I can't believe there's a Touron on the HMS *Pogue*. Part of me expects the boat to throw her overboard, spitting her out like a sour cherry.

"I didn't ask you to chase after me," Savannah says. "In fact, I literally just said that I wish you hadn't."

"Excuse me for trying to help!" I shout, throwing up my arms the way my dad does when he's had enough of me. But I notice that her hands are trembling, wrapped around the beer can. She sees me staring and quickly takes a swig, gripping the can tighter.

"Why don't we all just make a pact to try to stay in the boats from now on?" John B says reasonably. "With all the blood in the water by now, you never know what might come along."

He has a point—between the fish I lost and the one Savannah lost, we might attract sharks.

"You guys had a near miss, too?" Savannah asks. Her tone is a lot friendlier when she's talking to John B than when she's talking to me. Guess she prefers guys who don't risk their lives for her.

"This one did," John B says, pointing at me. "Sucker tried to drag him away, just like you."

Savannah shakes her head. "Not just like me. Nothing *dragged* me anywhere. I jumped."

"Oh, so you were the one calling the shots in the water?" I ask angrily, but Savannah just shrugs.

Her nonchalance is the most annoying thing about her. Stupid Kooks never have to worry about anything.

"Did you really think being rich would protect you from drowning? Like you could somehow, I don't know, *buy* your safety? I hate to tell you, honey, but that fish doesn't accept American Express."

Savannah looks at me witheringly. "What I *thought* was that I'm the captain of my swim team at school and an experienced spear-fisher who knew exactly what she was doing. *You* assumed I didn't."

I try to come up with a clever retort but find myself speechless. I guess I shouldn't be surprised that she's a competitive swimmer; she swam to the *Pogue* much faster than I did. Savannah tilts her head up to the sun and closes her eyes. What is she, like working on her tan? She needs to get back to her own boat. John B and I came out here to take a break from Kook-landia, not to join it.

Finally, her boyfriend pulls their fancy rental boat up alongside the *Pogue*.

"Savannah!" Hunter calls out. "Are you okay?"

"Fine!" Savannah says, then jerks a finger in my direction. "This kid nearly drowned himself, though."

"I did not!" I shout, but Savannah ignores me.

"Will you toss me my phone, Hunter?"

"There's no service out here," Hunter points out reasonably.

"Yeah, but I want to take a picture of myself on this boat. This'll make a great story when we get back to Charleston."

One of the Touron girls behind Hunter giggles, like the idea of Savannah on a boat as beat up as ours is some kind of joke.

"Where's your phone?" Hunter asks.

"My jeans pocket. In my tote. Just toss me the whole thing."

Hunter picks up a canvas tote bag from the deck of the boat and tosses it across the water. Savannah checks the pockets of her jeans but comes up empty-handed. Beneath us, I can feel the waves lifting and dropping the *Pogue*. The water's not smooth and glassy like it was when we got here. Savannah and her friends don't seem to notice.

"Must be in my sweatshirt pocket," Savannah mutters, digging out a sweatshirt from the bottom of the bag. She pulls her phone from the front pocket and takes a selfie, smiling brightly.

"Well"—I gesture to the other boat—"I guess it's time for you to get going."

Savannah doesn't move. After a moment, she says, "But I just promised your friend here that I'd stay out of the water for the rest of the day." She smiles in John B's direction. "What if I slipped and fell in when I tried to jump from one boat to the other? How many times can you jump into the water to save me?"

She flutters her eyelashes like now she's playing a damsel in distress. I roll my eyes.

"Hey, Hunt!" one of the other Touron guys calls out. "Can we get out of here already?"

"Yeah," the girl who giggled agrees. "This is boring and I'm freezing."

She's freezing? She's not the one who's soaking wet.

"Savannah," Hunter shouts. "I think we should get going."

"How can they be bored?" Savannah asks, and for a second she reminds me of John B, the sort of person who can't imagine that it's even possible to get bored on the water. "We're in the middle of one of the most dangerous and exciting spots on the Atlantic Ocean."

One of Hunter's douchey friends chimes in. "You call this exciting? Let's get back to the hot tub at the hotel. *That's* exciting." He winks at one of the girls on board and she giggles. "Come on, Hunt," he adds, "get your girl in line. Bad enough she wouldn't let us call the cops on these guys."

I face Savannah, surprised. "Winning a bet seemed like more fun than watching you two get arrested," she explains with a shrug.

"Come on, Savannah," Hunter says, his voice suddenly harsh, "I think we've humored you and your strange hobbies long enough."

Humored her? By, like, doing something she wanted to do? And spearfishing isn't a strange hobby, it's a way of life, going back literally millennia. I turn back to Savannah, waiting for her to say exactly that, but she keeps quiet. Then Hunter holds out his hand and snaps his fingers like he's calling a dog to heel.

Okay, she definitely isn't going to keep quiet about *that*, right?

Hunter drops his voice, but I can hear it when he says, "Don't embarrass me like you did last night, running through the hotel over a bottle of champagne like I couldn't afford to replace it."

Hunter thought that was *embarrassing*? I mean, I was the one getting chased, but even I have to admit what she did was badass.

I'm done keeping my mouth shut. "Hang on a sec—me, jumping into the water to save your life is treating you like a helpless fairy-tale princess, but this guy *snapping* his fingers at you is okay?"

John B puts his hand on my arm. "It's none of our business, JJ," he says softly. "Let's just be glad these guys are getting out of here and we can get back to fishing."

Another wave lifts the *Pogue* beneath us. I hate to admit it, but the water's getting too choppy for spearfishing—we won't be able to see the fish beneath us.

Savannah puts her beer down. She slips her tote bag over her shoulder and stands to make the jump, but just as she does a swell rises beneath us, pushing the two boats so close together that they rapidly bump into each other and then apart. I lose my balance, falling to my knees. Savannah drops alongside me, her bare feet sliding over the deck.

If she'd jumped into the water then, she might have been crushed between the boats.

Big John always used to say that out on the water, weather doesn't work like it does on land. Conditions can change in a heartbeat. I never knew exactly what he meant.

Now I get it.

The sky darkens as clouds cover the sun. The small, choppy waves beneath us grow bigger.

Another swell rises beneath us, picking up our boat and letting it fall so quickly that it feels like my stomach jumps up to my throat and then back down again. Savannah bumps into me. I can feel her shivering.

I'm cold, too, still soaked from jumping in after her. My teeth start to chatter.

Somehow, John B is still on his feet, and he's got his hands on his hips. Above us, he yells, "I thought you said the weather forecast was perfect, JJ."

CHAPTER 13

JOHN B

"WE'VE GOTTA GET OUT OF HERE, SAVANNAH," THAT GUY Hunter shouts. "Looks like that storm changed direction after all."

"What storm?" I look at JJ. I'm shouting now, too. With the wind picking up, it's too loud not to.

Savannah and JJ stand up carefully, balancing their arms against each other. The water is choppy beneath us. Savannah moves to the edge of the boat and lifts her foot like she's about to jump.

"What are you thinking?" JJ yells, grabbing her arm and pulling her backward. "You could get crushed to death."

"Let's get out of here, Hunt!" one of the Kook guys shouts.

"Come on, Savannah," Hunter calls. "Now."

Savannah shakes off JJ's grip. She looks from Hunter to JJ like she's not sure what's worse—getting crushed between the two boats or being stuck on the *Pogue* with us.

I silently add getting crushed between two boats to my list of ways to die on the water.

"If you're gonna go," I say finally, "better do it now, before conditions get worse."

JJ looks at me like I suggested she jump in the water with a weight tied around her waist.

"What are you talking about, John B?" he moans. "There's, like, a two percent chance of making that jump safely. Don't jump, Savannah."

Savannah looks at him icily. "Don't tell me what to do," she says firmly.

"Now, Savannah," Hunter shouts again.

"Now who's telling you what to do?" JJ asks.

"Hunter's my boyfriend," Savannah says, like that gives him the right to talk to her however he wants, even if it's putting her life in danger.

The sky opens up and it starts to rain. Without the sun overhead, it's as dark as twilight. On Hunter's boat, the Tourons squeal and make their way below deck.

"We gotta go, Hunt!" one of the guys calls as he grabs their cooler and brings it inside, like losing their beer is the biggest thing he has to worry about.

Hunter gives his friend a thumbs-up and turns back to the *Pogue*. "Come on, Savannah. You don't want to get stuck on the water with those two."

"What's that supposed to mean?" JJ scoffs. "She's safer with us than she would be with someone who doesn't even know how to hold a speargun, let alone navigate a storm."

Hunter sneers. "Like that piece-of-shit boat is safer than this one."

"With the right captain at the helm, it absolutely is," JJ counters, gesturing to me. I can't help it, I feel myself swell with pride at the compliment. I think, again, of all the things my dad taught me about being safe on the water.

Then again, lesson number one was probably "Check the weather." Which I definitely didn't do this time around. JJ said he did, but I should've known better. Not that I should've known JJ was lying—though it's not exactly surprising; once he gets an idea to do something in his head, he's not about to let something like the weather stop him—but because this is my boat. It's my job to double-check everything.

I should've checked the weather myself.

But I didn't. Because just like JJ, I didn't want anything to stop us from leaving the OBX behind today. I didn't want to spend another day, another night, in that house, waiting for the sound of my dad opening the door only to be met with silence.

"Savannah," Hunter says like her name is a warning. (If JJ or I ever talked to Kiara in that tone, she'd kick the shit out of us.) "Our friends are waiting for you."

"Let them wait!" JJ shouts. "She's gonna get herself killed, making that jump."

I can't tell if it bothers Savannah more that Hunter is telling her to jump or that JJ is telling her not to. Finally, she moves to the railing again, preparing to jump.

"Savannah, what are you doing?" JJ says, and he sounds genuinely scared.

"Come on, Savannah," Hunter shouts, and JJ looks at Hunter with daggers in his eyes.

Before Savannah can make the jump, the water beneath us shifts again, driving the boats farther apart. The rain is storming down. Savannah loses her balance and falls backward, sending her tote flying across the base of the *Pogue*. JJ catches her, but she shrugs off his touch again.

I can see Hunter is shouting something, but I can't hear him anymore. It's impossible to hear anything that's not the sound of rain slamming down onto the *Pogue*'s deck. He makes a bunch of gestures—at us, at the sky, at the water below. Then he starts turning his boat around and heading back the way he came.

Savannah turns to me. "Let's get out of here," she says. JJ looks at me and nods.

You don't have to tell me twice.

✳ ✳ ✳

Even though it's raining, Savannah changes out of her wetsuit (she's wearing a bathing suit underneath) and into her jeans and sweatshirt. She pulls her hood up over her head and crouches at the bow of the boat. JJ comes to stand beside me, holding on to the side of the boat for balance as we bounce over the waves. Between the rain falling down and the chop beneath us, I lose my grip on the boat's controls for a second. JJ is quick to take hold until I steady myself.

"I thought she was going to jump," he says to me, standing close enough that he can keep his voice low so Savannah won't overhear us. "Didn't you?"

I nod. "Hunter was more worried about how it would look to his friends if she stayed with a couple of Pogues than whether she'd risk her life to get back to his boat."

"Exactly," JJ agrees. "But what I don't get is, why would a girl like that be with such a creep?"

"Girls date creeps all the time," I answer with a shrug.

"Yeah, but you'd think the kind of girl who'll run through a hotel lobby to catch a thief wouldn't."

"Apparently running through the hotel lobby pissed off her boyfriend," I point out.

"All the more reason you'd think a girl like that wouldn't be with that kind of guy."

JJ says *a girl like that* with actual admiration in his voice. "JJ, are you *blushing*?" I tease. The thing is, even though that first version of Savannah—the fearless girl—couldn't stop arguing with JJ, I've also never seen anyone who reminded me so much of him.

"Shut up." JJ tries to sound exasperated, but I can tell he's embarrassed. "I was just gonna say that she seems to like you a lot better than she likes me."

I shake my head. "Only because I wasn't the one yelling at her nonstop."

"I wasn't yelling at her," JJ insists. "But would it have killed her to thank me for saving her life?"

I've never seen JJ this bent out of shape about a girl, even Kiara. When Kie gives him a hard time and rejects his attempts at flirting, JJ always laughs it off. But he's definitely not laughing about Savannah. I glance back at her to make sure she's not listening to us. She's still crouched in the front of the boat. I don't think she'd be able to hear us over the sound of the rain anyhow.

"JJ and Savannah, sittin' in a tree," I sing-song, and JJ shoves me. I laugh. "Hey, man, don't hit the guy who's trying to navigate our way back home safely." Even though I'm teasing JJ, I'm also hanging on to the boat's controls so tightly that my knuckles are white. It's gotten so dark and the rain is so heavy that I can barely see ahead of us.

"We gonna be okay?" JJ asks, his voice turning serious.

"Sure," I say, but I sound more confident than I feel. I tap the side of the boat. "The *Pogue*'s been through worse than this."

"I'm sorry I didn't check the weather," JJ says, surprising me. "That was a dick move."

"I should've checked, too," I answer finally.

"You mean you should've known better than to get on a boat with an idiot like me without double-checking to make sure I wasn't lying?" I can tell that JJ wants his question to be a joke, but he sounds pained.

"No, I mean, it was just as irresponsible for me to take the boat out without checking the forecast as for you. We're in this together."

JJ nods. "Let's get to work," he says finally.

CHAPTER 14

JJ

I RUSH AROUND THE *POGUE*, TYING DOWN ANYTHING THAT might blow away in the wind or that might roll overboard as the waves tip and toss the boat. The water is so choppy I have to drop to my hands and knees to make it from one side of the boat to the other. John B stays at the wheel, trying to direct us in and around the chop. The boat bounces so that even on my knees, I lose my balance.

Through the rain, I see Savannah huddled in the bow of the boat, sitting cross-legged with a rain-soaked towel over her shoulders. I crawl over to her.

"You must be freezing," I say.

I'm trying to be nice, but it must not translate into Kook girl language, because Savannah sounds insulted when she says, "No more than you."

"Well, I am cold," I say truthfully.

I mean, we both jumped into the water, and neither of us had a chance to really dry off before the rain started. And at least I have shoes on. Savannah's feet are bare.

I don't get this girl. I mean, I really, really don't get her.

She's tough enough to run after us through a fancy hotel, bold enough to dive into the water after a fish—but she was going to risk her life because her boyfriend told her to.

I can't stop myself from asking, "Why are you dating such a creep?"

More than once, Kiara has told me I should *stop and think* before I open my big mouth. I always roll my eyes when she says it—what's so great about being careful? And anyway, isn't Kiara the one who says we shouldn't censor ourselves? But she also says that being thoughtful and respectful isn't the same thing as censorship.

Right now, for the first time, I wish I'd mastered Kiara's whole "think before I talk" thing. Because Savannah's face looks like I just, I don't know, really hurt her feelings. But then her expression shifts into something else—instead of hurt, she looks pissed.

"You don't even know Hunter," she says.

"I know he acted like you embarrassed him just because you wanted to go fishing."

"He did not! He wanted to go fishing, too."

I think of the way he held his speargun. "Didn't look like he did. And then he left you alone on the water in a serious storm."

"You were the one trying to stop me from jumping back to his boat!"

Savannah's eyes are light brown, and they look almost reddish when she's angry.

"Yeah, but that still doesn't mean he should've just left you here," I say.

"What was he supposed to do? Tag along after your boat through the storm?"

"Of course not," I answer.

"Then what?" Savannah asks.

The truth is, I can't come up with an answer.

Savannah continues: "Seems to me that you're the creep, judging Hunter when you don't even know him."

I shake my head. "I don't have to know him. He's a mainland Kook. Meet one, you've met them all."

"What's a Kook?" Savannah asks.

"You know, a rich kid. Someone spoiled who's never had to work a day in their life. Unlike us—John B and me—we're Pogues."

"I thought this *boat* was the *Pogue*."

"That's *why* we call it that."

"You named your boat after an insult?"

"It's John B's boat. And it's not an insult. I'd rather be a Pogue than a Kook. Pogues are the lowest fish on the food chain—you know, the runts that fishermen toss back into the ocean, can't even be bothered to kill them."

"That's what you want to be?"

"That's what I *am*. Pogues are survivors. Everything Kooks have has been handed to them."

"So is that the real reason you wanted me to get on Hunter's boat? You didn't want to be stuck with a Kook like me during the storm?"

"What?" I say. The wind is howling so I have to yell. John B shouts something, but it's too loud to hear him and the boat takes a sudden nosedive into the belly of a wave. Savannah and I fall forward. John B's and my spearguns are barreling toward us—I must not have tied them down properly.

Shit.

I reach for Savannah's arm, trying to move us out of the path of the spears with their sharp tips, but before I can, Savannah leans over me, catches the spears in one hand, and ties them down tight with the other.

The boat rights itself. The water remains choppy, but the waves aren't so giant (yet) that the skiff can't float over them.

"Where'd you learn to do that?" I ask, impressed.

Savannah flashes her fiery eyes at me. "What, you think a Kook can't tie a knot?"

I shrug. It's not just a knot, though. It's the sort of nautical knot that Big John taught John B and me on our fishing trips back in the day.

"You think they're okay out there?" Savannah says suddenly, her eyes softening.

"Who?" I ask dumbly.

"Who?" Savannah echoes. "Hunter! Our friends! This is all my fault. I'm the one who wanted to get out on the water. We knew that there was a storm offshore, but I was positive we'd be able to steer clear, so I convinced Hunter there was nothing to worry about. He's not as experienced on the water as I am, and now they're stuck out here."

"I knew it," I say. "Hunter has no idea what he's doing on the water, does he?"

"Shut up," Savannah says, but she looks more frightened than angry.

"I'm sorry," I say solemnly. Hunter may be a jerk, but he and his friends are navigating this storm just like we are. "I'm sure they're fine." I'm a little surprised to hear myself trying to reassure this girl. "Boats like that have such fancy nav systems, they practically drive themselves."

Savannah nods, but I can tell she's not entirely convinced.

I could tell her that I know how she feels.

Not, obviously, the being worried about some creep part, but the feeling like it's all her fault.

Because it's my fault John B and I are out here now.

I'm the one who didn't check the weather, and even if I did, I would've rationalized the storm away, just like Savannah did.

But it's more than the weather—this *whole trip* was my idea.

I thought this was the best way to get John B's mind off his dad, but all I've done is remind John B of Big John. Fishing, driving a boat—that's all stuff we learned from Big John.

And now we're in this storm, and I'm the one who can't stop thinking about Big John. What if Big John got caught on the water in conditions like this—or worse? His boat probably didn't have a state-of-the-art navigation system like Hunter's, and even if it did, no matter what I said—the best nav system in the world is no match for a killer storm.

Boats go missing on the water all the time. Even enormous ships get lost or stuck.

I look up at John B, standing at the controls, hanging on for dear life. He looks so determined—he looks just like his dad. A crack of lightning illuminates the sky above us, followed seconds later by a deafening roar of thunder.

"Shit!" John B shouts, and I get to my feet and make my way over to him.

"What's wrong?"

John B manages to smile even as he's shaking his head. "You mean other than the fact that we're in the Graveyard of the Atlantic during a major storm?" he asks.

"Yeah, other than that," I answer.

John B's smile vanishes as his face turns serious, as serious as I've ever seen. "The engine died."

CHAPTER 15

JOHN B

WHAT WOULD DAD DO? WHAT WOULD DAD DO? AS SOON AS I EVEN think the question another question pops into my brain: *What* did *Dad do?*

Did he get caught in a storm like this?

Did he die *in a storm like this?*

I scrub the thought from my mind even as I try to restart the engine. Nobody is better on the water than my dad. I'm just freaking out 'cause we're stuck here. It has nothing to do with Dad. He'd never be so stupid, to get caught on the water without checking the weather radars first. He'd have paid attention to the radar, avoided storms.

And if he absolutely couldn't avoid bad weather—well, he'd find a safe place to ride out the storm.

And that's exactly what *we're* going to do now.

The light tower on the southern edge of the shoals. Like I told JJ, I've been there once—not up inside, but Dad took me there on one of our fishing trips. He loved the light tower, though I thought it looked like a rusty old mess on stilts. Dad told me the light tower is famous because it's survived several significant tropical storms and that the tower marks the edge of the shoals at the confluence of the Cape Fear River and the Atlantic Ocean. It hasn't been used as an actual lighthouse in years. It's not shaped like a normal lighthouse but, Dad explained, like a steel oil-drilling platform, a "Texas tower" on top of four steel legs. I remember the four steel posts holding it up over the water—posts with rusted rungs nailed into them, so anyone could tie off their boat and climb up to the tower above.

If the light tower could survive all those storms, right smack at the edge of the Graveyard of the Atlantic, it can survive *this* storm. Which means, if we can get there, *we* can survive this storm.

JJ bends over the engine at the back of the boat while I stay at the controls. He uses his body to shield it from the rain.

"Flooded!" JJ shouts, which means the spark plugs are too wet to spark.

Savannah holds an enormous torch of a flashlight over him. (At least we remembered to bring *that*.)

JJ engages the choke—a small valve in the carburetor to reduce the amount of air added to the fuel. You can engage the choke to give it a boost of fuel, which is sometimes enough to make it turn, but you have to be careful to disengage the choke immediately to keep the engine from flooding all over again, as too much fuel is pumped into the cylinders. JJ is much better at these sorts of things than I am.

"Try again," JJ shouts over the wind, pulling at the engine. I try the controls; nothing happens. JJ leans down again. A few minutes later he shouts, "Now!"

This time the engine starts. JJ cheers and Savannah lifts her arms overhead like she's just run a race. For a second, I think they're going to actually hug.

I point us in the direction of the light tower. I have no idea whether it will be empty. Dad told me it used to be a bed and breakfast, and it's privately owned these days.

JJ makes his way across the boat to me, walking with his knees bent for balance. He puts a hand on my shoulder. "What's the plan?"

"Light tower," I say. JJ nods; he doesn't need me to explain. Most of the lessons my dad taught me, he taught JJ, too.

"I'll keep an eye on the engine," JJ says. "You just get us there."

I've been on the water in choppy conditions before, but I've never rode through anything like this. At times, it's like we're in a canyon between monster waves; and then suddenly we're on the top of a crest, and nothing I do at the controls matters—all I can do is hope that when the wave crashes, we'll still be right side up.

Through the rain, I see JJ wrapping Savannah in a life vest, and then handing her a rope; she ties herself to the side of the boat. Without a word, JJ ties a vest around my shoulders, a rope around my waist, then does the same thing to himself.

Since the light tower isn't actually in use, the light in the lighthouse won't be lit. Which means it'll be all but impossible to see in the darkness. Which means I could be sending the boat directly toward it—we could literally be smashed to bits against one of those steel legs.

I could kill us all.

Maybe this brilliant plan of mine wasn't so brilliant after all.

But suddenly, a bolt of lightning cuts through the sky, brightening the world around us.

"There it is!" I shout. JJ takes the heavy-duty flashlight and points toward the tower. I follow its beam.

The tower hasn't changed since I came here with Dad: four steel legs with a two-level platform on top. And on one corner of the platform, there's a tall, skinny lighthouse.

One of the four legs has a rusty-looking staircase spiraling down it. I get as close to it as I can.

"JJ!" I command. He takes my place at the controls, and I grab another rope and secure one end to the boat. I have to tie us to one of the tower's metal rungs.

I'm going to have to jump.

Not too long ago, Savannah was trying to jump between our boat and Hunter's and I thought she might get herself killed. But that jump wasn't nearly this long, and even though the waves were choppy, they were nothing like *this*.

I look back at JJ—I can't make out the expression on his face, but he knows what I have to do. Savannah holds the flashlight, trying to keep the light steady on the ladder rungs. I take a deep breath.

I jump.

"Got it!" I shout triumphantly as my fingers wrap around the wet metal. But before I can tie off the rope, the metal snaps beneath my hands, rusted through.

"Shit!" I scramble as I drop, grabbing for another rung. This one holds fast.

JJ steers as best he can, and I tie the boat, tight, at both ends. It's as close to the tower as it's gonna get, but he and Savannah are going to have to jump, too.

I pull myself onto the spiraling stairs, lying flat on my stomach with my arms outstretched, ready to catch them if I have to.

I can't hear Savannah and JJ on the boat, but it looks like they're arguing about who's going to jump first. JJ must win, because soon Savannah hands him the flashlight and perches on the edge of the boat. I reach out my arms.

Savannah leaps. She catches the same rung where I tied off the rope and pulls herself up. (She didn't need me to help her. Maybe she could have jumped to Hunter's boat after all.)

I gesture for JJ to toss me the flashlight. I catch it, then aim the light back at JJ, so he'll be able to see where he's aiming.

JJ walks around the *Pogue* one more time, checking that everything that can be tied down is.

Then he positions himself on the bow of the boat and springs.

He hits the steel leg of the tower with such a hard smack that the stairs shudder beneath me. I drop the flashlight in the water below.

"JJ!" I shout, blind without the light.

Savannah echoes my shouts. "JJ!"

I can feel him moving on the steel leg of the tower, and I breathe a sigh of relief. He may be struggling, but at least he made it without falling into the water.

After what feels like forever, JJ scrambles up beside Savannah and me. "Shit!" he shouts. "The rung broke off in my hand."

"Which rung?" I shout back, hoping it's not one of the ones I tied the *Pogue* to. If the boat gets loose, then we're screwed. Even after the weather calms down, we'll be trapped here.

"I'm not sure," JJ answers.

Savannah reaches into her pocket to pull out her phone for its flashlight but I stop her. "Save the battery," I say. Whether the *Pogue* is safely attached to the tower doesn't make a difference right now. Now that all three of us are safely on the tower, we have to stay here till the storm is through. But we do have to get inside safely, and without the big flashlight, our phones are all we have.

"Good idea," JJ says, as Savannah tucks her phone into her pocket.

I get to my feet, holding on to the railing for dear life. My heart is pounding so hard that I swear it's louder than the thunder or the wind or the rain.

"Let's go," I say, leading the way up the spiraling stairs.

CHAPTER 16

JOHN B

THE STAIRS ARE RICKETY AND RUSTY, SHAKING IN THE wind. I hold tight and remind myself just how many storms—like serious hurricanes—this tower and these stairs have survived. When Dad brought me here, he recited all kinds of facts and made me say them back until I had them memorized, the same way he'd taught me about fishing and swimming and boat engines. So I know that the tower was built in 1966 and was manned by a four-person crew, twenty-four hours a day, seven days a week. The light got automated sometime in the 1970s, and Dad sounded kind of sad when he told me that, because all those people lost their jobs, I guess, and maybe because he liked the idea of working in a light tower someday or something.

"Why do you know so much about the tower, Dad?" I had asked.

Dad looked at me like he couldn't believe I hadn't figured it out already. "Because anything that survives this long on the water is downright fascinating."

Dad told me the tower was decommissioned altogether in 2004, when GPS systems on boats rendered the lighthouse obsolete.

They weren't thinking about boats like the *Pogue* that don't have sophisticated GPS systems.

Anyway, that means the Frying Pan Shoals light tower has survived literally every storm that's hit it since 1966. Hurricanes Florence, Irene, Sandy, and more. After all that, tonight's storm should be a cakewalk for this place, right?

When we reach the platform, I pull out my phone and turn on its flashlight. There's another set of stairs that leads to the next level, where the main structure is. There's a flat, sort of squat square building running the length of the platform with a railed deck around it; one corner is taken up by the decommissioned lighthouse.

The first door we try is locked. So is the next. JJ paces the length of the platform, trying one door after the next, but they're all locked.

I consider our options—we could stay outside, crouch as close to the building as we can to stay (kind of) dry, or we could break in.

Before I can make up my mind, I hear the sound of glass shattering. I look up and see that JJ wrapped his fist with his sweatshirt and literally punched a hole in a window. JJ's not the sort of person who stops to weigh his options before acting.

"What the hell?" Savannah shouts.

"Shit, JJ," I yell, but the truth is, I'm relieved JJ acted on impulse. Decision made. He climbs through the broken window and walks to the nearest door and unlocks it from inside. Savannah and I rush through the door. JJ slams it shut behind us.

"You didn't have to slam the door!" I say, feeling rattled.

"And you didn't have to break the glass without warning us first," Savannah adds. She stands on her tiptoes, careful to walk around the glass with her bare feet.

JJ shrugs. "It got us inside, didn't it? And anyway, the gale force winds out there slammed the door, not me."

Holding his phone out in front of him, JJ circles the room like a cat in a cage. He tries every light switch he sees, but nothing turns on.

"Doesn't this place have a generator?" JJ mutters.

I shrug. "Guess it's out of juice."

The room we're in is large and square. There are some worn couches arranged in one corner, a table and chairs in the other.

"This must have been the lobby when this place was a B&B," I try. It's nothing like the hotel we ran through last night. People probably didn't come here for a luxurious experience—they were here for the adventure maybe, or the isolation of being thirty-five miles off the coast of North Carolina. Maybe, like my dad, they liked the idea of working at a lighthouse and played pretend while they stayed here.

We follow the beam of JJ's phone into another room. Even though this room doesn't have any windows, I can still hear the wind howling outside.

JJ's light lands on a beat-up old pool table. Torn American flags hang on a wall behind it.

"Why do you think those flags are so ripped up?" JJ asks.

"Remember Hurricane Florence, a while back?" Savannah asks. "I forgot about it until just now, but there was a livestream online somewhere, and you could see the American flag on the Frying Pan tower being torn to shreds as the hurricane approached. People nicknamed the flag something silly—"

"Kevin," I supply. I remember watching the livestream with Dad. After the storm passed, the flag was recovered and sold at auction to raise money for the Red Cross.

"Maybe these are the flags that didn't go viral," Savannah guesses. "Like, they all flew on the tower, and as soon as the wind ripped one up too much, they'd replace it with a fresh flag and hang the old flag down here."

"Good guess," JJ says, and I look at him sideways, surprised that he's given her a compliment. JJ leads us to what must have been one of the guest rooms—there are two narrow twin beds, neatly made, like they're waiting for two little kids to slide between the sheets. In the next room there's (I think) a king-sized bed. JJ puts his phone down and flops onto the bed, wrinkling the blankets. The metal bed frame squeaks beneath him. There's no big, fancy headboard like at Savannah's hotel last night. I guess they couldn't exactly lug enormous pieces of heavy furniture out here. In one corner of the room is a metal desk. I open up the drawers, looking for I don't know what, but they're all empty.

"This place is creepy," Savannah says finally. She's standing in the doorway, like she doesn't want to come all the way inside. "Did people really *pay* to stay here?"

I shrug. "Apparently."

"Not quite the lap of luxury you're used to," JJ adds, and Savannah tosses him an irritated look.

"You don't know what I'm used to," she says, but her words are drowned out by a bigger, louder noise. Something crashing.

JJ springs off the bed and lands in a crouch. Savannah jumps inside the doorway.

"It was probably just the wind, knocking something over," I suggest. "With that broken window in the front room, right?"

"Right," JJ says, even though we both know that the sound—whatever it was—sounded like it came from the lighthouse above us. "Probably. You're sure this place is empty, right?"

I look up like if I stare hard enough, I'll be able to see through the ceiling into the lighthouse above us. "I mean, my dad told me it's abandoned. I think the owners were trying to sell it, or have it declared a national landmark, or something. Maybe turn it into a museum." Dad knew what he was talking about, right? He was an expert on these sorts of things.

I realize, suddenly, that I'm thinking about him in the past tense. Silently, I repeat myself, like I think I can undo my thoughts: Dad *knows* what he's talking about. Dad *is* an expert.

"You know, they say this place is haunted." JJ puts on a spooky voice. "I mean, they don't call the shoals the Graveyard of the Atlantic for nothing."

I look at JJ angrily, wishing he wouldn't mention graveyards right now. Then I shake myself. It's not JJ's fault. It's not like he knows what's going on inside my head.

Still, I feel tense as he holds his phone in front of his face like we're sitting around a campfire telling ghost stories. "Whoooo," he says, "Fee-fi-fo-fum, I smell the blood of a Pogue-ish-man." I wish he would shut up.

"That's the giant from 'Jack and the Beanstalk,' " Savannah corrects. "Not a ghost." But her voice is shaking.

I look inside the closet—empty. I don't believe in ghosts. (At least, I don't think I do.) But it *is* true that over the centuries, hundreds of people died in Frying Pan Shoals, maybe even thousands. Some of their boats probably went down before they even realized what was happening. I picture passengers on luxury liners, asleep in the beds of their staterooms, waking up only when the water was around their ears and it was too late to even try to escape. I picture crews on wooden ships, settlers bound for the American colonies, fighting with all their might to keep their ships afloat, thinking of their families back in England, wondering if anyone would remember them after they were gone.

I think of lone fisherman, *Old Man and the Sea*-type stories—men trying to haul in a big catch to feed their families and getting stranded.

I think of explorers, trying to map these waters, long before we had radars and GPS and lighthouses to show them the way.

And I think of my dad. I picture him all alone on a little boat like the *Pogue*, battling a storm, fighting for his life. Fighting to get home to me.

All of this blips through my mind in a matter of seconds.

The sound of Savannah yelping interrupts my thoughts. JJ is chasing her around the room, moaning in what I assume he thinks is a good impersonation of a ghost's cry.

"Stop it, JJ," Savannah shouts, but she's laughing.

"Fee-fi-fo-fum," JJ repeats, holding his arms out like he's going to grab her.

"JJ! Chill!" I hold up my arm. Savannah stops short. JJ practically runs into her. I see the surprise on his face, and I can tell he never thought he was actually going to catch her. Now that he's standing right next to her, he drops his arms to his sides awkwardly.

My thoughts are racing, and I try to gather them.

1. I got caught in a storm and sought refuge in this light tower.

2. My dad taught me about this abandoned light tower when he brought me here on one of our fishing trips.

3. Was he trying to tell me something back then?

4. Before my dad vanished six months ago, he told me he might have to disappear for a while.

I sought refuge in the light tower because that's what my dad would have done. Because he taught me everything I know. Because I'm just like him.

"Did you hear that?" I ask.

"How could you hear anything over JJ's nonsense?" Savannah asks.

"It's not nonsense," JJ says, mock seriously. "I'm just showing the ghosts some respect by trying to speak their language."

"Shut up," I say. JJ must hear that I'm serious, because he finally keeps quiet.

There's a sound coming from above us again. But this isn't a crash. And it isn't the wind howling, either. This is different; it almost sounds like someone is up above us, their footsteps shuffling across the floor.

Maybe we're not the only ones seeking shelter here.

Maybe—maybe my dad is up there. Maybe he's been here for *weeks*. Maybe *this* is where he disappeared to, and he's been waiting for me to figure it out. Maybe that's why he made me memorize all those facts about this place, so I'd know exactly where to come and find him. Maybe he tied his boat off during a storm, just like we did, but maybe his boat floated away because whatever he was tied to rusted into rot. Maybe—

I can't wait. Before I know what I'm doing, I'm rushing back into the lobby, looking for the stairs that lead up to the lighthouse.

CHAPTER 17

JOHN B

IN ONE CORNER OF THE LOBBY, THERE'S A DOOR THAT LEADS to a narrow hallway lined with closets, and at the end of the hallway is a door that opens to reveal an even narrower staircase up into the lighthouse—a tall, square building that looks more like one of those air traffic control towers at the airport than the pictures of whitewashed lighthouses I've seen in Dad's old nautical books. I race up the stairs until I reach the top, where there's a control room with an enormous (unlit) light at its center, covered in glass panels.

I pace around the space, peering into every corner.

"There's no one here," I say, panting. Behind me, JJ is just as out of breath as I am, though Savannah is barely winded.

Savannah sees JJ and me looking at her, impressed. "Told you guys—captain of my swim team," she says, like that explains why she hasn't broken a sweat.

A gust of wind rattles the lighthouse, and the source of the noise we heard is revealed: a short metal file cabinet on wheels that rolls across the room every time the wind blows hard, occasionally crashing into one of the walls.

"You know, I read once that they actually design buildings to move in the wind," Savannah says, "so they can sustain the movement instead of just toppling over. Like, in California, they design tall buildings to be a little bit flexible, in case of earthquakes."

"I don't think anyone was worried about an earthquake when they built this place," JJ points out, but Savannah shrugs.

"I'm just saying, maybe they designed this place with the wind in mind. Better than flying off like Dorothy in *The Wizard of Oz*."

"*The Wizard of Oz*?" JJ echoes. "What are you even talking about?"

I can't pay attention to their bickering. I circle the round room until I'm dizzy. Finally I shout, "Shit!" and grab the file cabinet, shoving it into the wall. It falls onto its side.

"What'd those drawers ever do to you?" JJ asks, but I don't laugh. I don't even smile. I'm breathing as hard as I did running up the stairs. Harder. I can't catch my breath at all.

"Were you hoping to find a ghost?" JJ asks, but then the smile fades from his face, replaced by a look of understanding.

"John B—" he begins, but I cut him off.

"Don't make fun of me," I pant.

"I'm not."

"It's not *that* out there. If he'd gotten caught in a storm, he might have come here for safe harbor, just like us."

"Sure."

"Don't patronize me, either."

"Just because he's not here doesn't mean—"

I cut him off again. "I know what it means."

"I mean, there's literally a whole ocean out there. This is just one safe place, right?"

"I know," I repeat, my voice thick and deep. I bend down to pick up the cabinet I knocked over seconds ago. But instead of setting it upright, I shove it down again.

"What are you two talking about?" Savannah asks.

JJ glances at me like he's waiting for me to answer, but I don't feel like explaining.

"John B's dad went missing on the water about six months ago."

"Oh my god. I'm so sorry—" Savannah begins, but I cut her off, too.

"Don't offer me, like, condolences as though he's dead."

Savannah steps back like I slapped her, but I don't care. I'm sick of caring about other people's feelings. However bad she feels, it's not one iota as bad as I feel right now.

I was stupid to wonder if he might be here tonight, to think that he was trying to send me a secret message when he taught me about this place. What was I thinking? Like JJ said, there's a whole ocean out there.

"Savannah didn't mean it like that," JJ says.

It's not like him to try to play peacemaker. Usually that's my job. JJ turns back to Savannah and explains, "There's been no trace of him. Not his body or his boat. So he might . . ." He pauses, glancing at me warily. "So he's still out there, somewhere."

I hate everything about JJ's explanation. I hate how he can sum up my father's absence in a few sentences, and I hate that he slipped and said the word *might* the same way my thoughts slipped into the past tense before.

Now, JJ says, "It doesn't mean anything that he's not here, John B. Come on, what were the chances anyway? One in a million? One in a billion?"

Suddenly, I am so, so sick of the sound of JJ's voice. I feel like he hasn't stopped talking since he showed up at the Chateau at dawn this morning with his harebrained fishing trip plan.

But it's not just today. I'm sick of the sound of his little-kid voice echoing in my memories, asking my dad if he could come fishing with us, asking my dad to teach him how to fix a flooded engine, asking my dad, asking my dad, asking *my* dad.

"This isn't some kind of joke, JJ." My own voice sounds lower than usual. Thicker somehow.

"I'm not making fun of you," JJ says, but he sounds surprised. That's what we do—we make fun of each other. We crack jokes. I've never told him not to before. I've never complained that he crossed the line.

"Just because you don't know what it's like to have a dad you'd actually miss—"

Now, JJ cuts me off. "What the hell is that supposed to mean?"

The muscles in my jaw feel tight, like if I bit down hard enough my teeth could literally break. I look at the faded bruise on JJ's face.

"You have a dad, even if he sucks—he's still your family. You don't know what it's like to be all alone. You don't know what it's like to care about another person. If your dad went missing, you'd probably throw a party to celebrate it. You'd never have to worry about his temper again, right?"

"What do you want me to say, John B, that the wrong dad went missing? You think I don't already think that, all the time? I've wished your dad was my dad half my life." JJ looks like he's going to cry, or hit something, or both.

But I don't try to make him feel better and I don't try to calm him down. Instead I say, "Yeah, no shit. That's what you were doing, all those mornings you showed up at my house, taking my dad's time and attention. You didn't care if you didn't have any family of your own, not when you could just steal mine."

I notice JJ's fingers curling into fists. Good, I think. Let him throw the first punch. Because right now, I feel like if I don't hit something, I'm going to explode.

CHAPTER 18

JJ

JOHN B'S NEVER TALKED TO ME LIKE THAT.

Only Luke—my dad—has ever talked to me like that.

I brace myself, like I think John B is going to hit me.

But I also feel my fingers twist into fists. I actually want to hit John B, my best friend.

The thing is, John B's not entirely wrong. I mean, I wouldn't exactly *celebrate* if my dad went missing, but I probably wouldn't miss him, either.

I'd be, I don't know, *relieved* to have a break from Luke. Relieved if I didn't have to hold my breath every time I walked into our house, wondering what kind of mood Dad is going to be in, wondering which thing I say is going to be the thing that sets him off.

Sometimes I think about fighting back—hitting him back.

But then I think he'll just get angrier.

Sometimes I think if I just do everything right, he'll never hurt me again.

But I have no idea how to do everything right.

I don't know how I'd feel if my dad was gone, like, *forever.* I mean, he's my dad. I'm supposed to love him.

But sometimes I think I hate him.

John B must notice my clenched fists because he shifts his stance, balancing on his heels like he's expecting a punch.

"What are you doing, JJ?" Savannah breaks in, and I blink—I forgot she was here. I look down and realize that I'm holding my fists up by my chest.

I take a breath and lower my fists. "I'm not like my dad," I say, and John B nods.

"I know that."

"I don't deal with problems by beating someone up."

"I know that, too."

I hate that Savannah is seeing this, hearing this. What goes on between me and my dad is none of anyone's business. Can she make out the shadow of a bruise on my face, a souvenir from Dad's latest smack?

This stupid trip was supposed to take our minds off our dads, but instead, it's like they're both here with us in this tiny control room.

I don't want Savannah feeling sorry for me.

And I don't want to hit John B, no matter how upset I am about what he said.

But I do want to hit *something.* And looking at John B, I can tell he does, too.

There's a control panel full of buttons and switches right in front of me—I hit it. I scream when my knuckles make contact with the metal—

that's how much it hurts. But I can't stop—I think it would hurt more to keep still.

So I take another punch, and then another.

After a minute, John B joins in, kicking the base of the enormous light in the center of the room. Soon we're both destroying these useless controls—buttons that have no juice, switches that haven't turned anything on in god knows how long.

And then, out of nowhere—light.

I mean, the enormous light in the center of the room flickers on, just for a second.

"Whoa," Savannah says. "How'd you do that?"

John B and I look at each other. Neither of us has any idea. It's not like we were keeping close track of which mechanics we were kicking the shit out of.

Suddenly, John B grins. And then he's laughing—and I am, too, so hard that my stomach hurts. Somehow, our fight, our temper tantrum—whatever you want to call it—revealed that this place isn't quite as out of juice as we thought.

And if we could make that light come on once—without even trying—then we can do it again.

Someone might see it and rescue us.

And even if no one sees, then at least we wouldn't have to make it through the night in pitch darkness, holding our breaths while we wait for the sun to come up, rationing our phones' flashlights to save their batteries.

John B and I high-five each other, hands no longer clenched. I crouch down over the control panel and get to work.

*** *** ***

I definitely don't get, you know, A's like Pope does, but there's one thing I'm better at than he is, better than Kiara, even better than John B: mechanics. Ever since I was little, I needed to know *how* things worked. It's why John B stayed at the wheel while I worked on the *Pogue*'s engine when it died.

When I started cutting school in fifth grade, I didn't just waste my time goofing off—I mean, I did that, too—but I'd also head to the local garage, hang out with the mechanics. Now, I can fix any car—an old one with a diesel engine, or something shiny and new, with inner workings that look more like a computer than an internal combustion engine.

When our school offered an elective course in mechanics, it was the one class I never missed—though sometimes it was so boring when the teacher droned on about the theory behind the inner workings of machines.

I'm not interested in theory.

I'm interested in actually *doing* things.

Anyway, if you have to be stuck in a decommissioned lighthouse, there's probably no one better to be stuck with than me.

If anyone has a chance of getting this thing up and running, it's me.

So now I'm crouched underneath the control panel, trying to see exactly which wire is attached to which control. I'm holding my phone in my mouth, angling the flashlight by biting down on it just right, while my hands trace the wires. John B is back down in the B&B part of the tower, looking for any food and water the old employees might have left behind.

"Let me do that." Savannah crawls under the panel with me—it's basically like a big metal desk above us—and pulls my phone from my mouth. She doesn't seem grossed out when she wipes off my saliva.

I adjust so that I'm lying on my back with the panel above me, and Savannah tucks herself in beside me.

"Better?" she asks, holding the light up.

"Much," I say.

Lucky for me, I'm the sort of person who can concentrate on more than one thing at a time. Which means I can stay totally focused on the wires overhead and just as focused on the warmth of Savannah's body next to me. Her hip presses against mine. Her clothes are damp, and I think she must be freezing.

If we were in an old movie, I would probably offer her my shirt or something. But the thing is, I'm cold, too.

Or anyway, I was before I started concentrating on the control panel.

And before Savannah crawled in next to me.

It's not like I've never been this close to a girl before. But this feels different. I can't figure Savannah out. She doesn't seem like just another Kook Touron.

I'm not sure what she seems like.

After a few minutes, I slide out from under the panel and stand looking down at the controls. I don't have to ask Savannah to follow—she just does it, holding the light up exactly where I need it.

"I don't need help," I say finally. "You could head back down with John B. There are blankets on those beds. You could warm up."

"And you could go back to holding the phone between your teeth." Savannah grins.

"That was working just fine!" I insist.

The wind blows so that the tower moves again, but Savannah doesn't look scared. I press a few buttons, and the light behind us flickers, then goes out again.

I shake my head. "I can't figure out why that sucker won't stay lit."

"Guess they had it right in the old days," Savannah says.

"What do you mean?"

"You know, back in the day that would've been a gas lamp, right?" Savannah gestures to the light in the center of the round room, encircled with dusty glass panels. "They wouldn't have needed to get the electricity up and running to light it. We could've just . . . lit a match or something."

"Do you have a match?" I ask.

Savannah shakes her head. "Even if I did, it'd be soaking wet."

"So, score one for electricity."

I expect Savannah to pout, but instead she laughs. "Good point."

I climb back under the panel, and Savannah follows with the light. Her wet hair brushes against my face. It smells like fancy shampoo. We're both on our hands and knees, and her pinkie finger bumps into mine.

"I have an idea," Savannah says. She puts my phone on the floor, the light facing up into the panel, then slides out and up to stand. "You plug that wire—"

"Which wire?"

"The green one," she says, like it's obvious which one she meant. "Anyway, you plug it into place when I flip the main breaker switch up here."

"Why?" I go to slide out after her, but instead I bump my head against the top of the control panel. The light flickers again.

Savannah laughs. "It's just an instinct. Like, if we can time it just right, it'll flood the system with power at the right moment."

"Like jump-starting a car."

"Exactly!"

"Like you've ever jump-started a car."

"What's that supposed to mean?"

"Don't people like you pay other people to do that sort of thing for them?"

"*People like me*?" Savannah echoes. "You sure make a lot of assumptions about my life when you don't even know me."

Okay, I admit it. She has me there.

Like I said, I haven't quite figured her out yet. Until tonight, I would've said, *You meet one Kook, you've met them all. Rich and problem-free.*

But Savannah doesn't seem like that. Certainly not right now, stranded on a light tower with John B and me. That definitely qualifies as a *problem*.

"Can we try it?" Savannah asks. "The jump-starting idea?"

I nod and crawl back under the panel. I grab the green wire and hold it over its plug.

"On the count of three," I begin. "One, two—"

"Three!" Savannah shouts, flipping the switch above me. I shove the wire into place.

All at once, the tower is flooded with light. Not just the lighthouse lamp in the center of the room, but the control panel lights up, too. I scramble to my feet, and before I know what's happening, Savannah's throwing her arms around me, covering me with the scent of her fruity-flowery shampoo and the surprising warmth of her fingers on the back of my neck.

"You did it, JJ!" she shouts triumphantly.

"We did it," I correct. I press my hands into her back, giving her a squeeze. "That was a great idea. How'd you know how to do that?"

Savannah pulls away, shrugging. "Like I said, just an instinct."

She turns the light on my phone off and holds it out to me, standing so far from me she has to hold her arm out straight. I put it into my pocket, wondering what I said wrong.

Before I can figure it out, I hear John B whooping from below.

"Guess he can see the light from down there," I say finally. "Let's go see if he had as much luck with food as we did with the light."

I head for the stairs. I hear Savannah take a deep breath before she follows me.

CHAPTER 19

JOHN B

ALMOST AS SOON AS THE LIGHT GOES ON, I SEE IT THROUGH the rain. A boat, bouncing over the chop below. Bigger than the *Pogue*—about the size of some of the big Kook yachts in the marina back home, though not nearly as nice. It's weaving its way between the waves, headed toward the tower. The closer it comes, the better I see her. She doesn't look like one of the Kook yachts in the marina back home. But she's not a little skiff like the *Pogue*, either. She's big. Not, like, official international shipping freighter or cruise ship big, but big enough.

Big enough to carry cargo.

"Yo, any luck? Did you find any food or drink down here?" JJ calls out as he comes down the stairs from the lighthouse and back into the lobby, Savannah behind him. I hold up my hand for them to be quiet, like I'm scared whoever's on that boat might hear us, all the way up here. JJ joins me at the window and follows my eyes down to the water.

"Guess we're not the only ones who thought this was a good place to ride out the storm," he says soberly.

"Guess not," I agree.

"Want me to cut the light?" JJ asks. I shake my head.

"If we turn it off now, they'll know there's someone here. If it just stays on, they'll think, I don't know, it's automated or something." I *hope* they'll think that.

"What should we do?" JJ asks.

"Why do you guys sound so worried?" Savannah cuts in. "What's wrong with someone else riding out the storm here? It's a safe place, right?"

I shake my head.

JJ, Savannah, and I are out here because we were unlucky. Shipping freighters would've gotten the storm warning from the Coast Guard and redirected. People like Hunter, cluelessly out on the water, have sophisticated nav systems to guide them home.

There's a chance that whoever's out there was just unlucky like we were. Just a few minutes ago, I was hoping that my dad might have come here to wait out the storm. But the truth is, the odds are that the only people who'd be out on a night like this, are people who don't want anyone to know they're out.

"What do you think?" JJ asks, dropping his voice to a whisper.

"As long as they tie their boat off on one of the other posts, we don't have to worry about them seeing the *Pogue* and figuring out anyone else is here."

Pope would say it's a one in four chance. Or a twenty-five percent chance. Maybe he'd, I don't know, sit down and make a graph or something to explain our odds of being caught.

"You two head back up to the lighthouse," I say finally. "With any luck, they'll just tie off their boat and hang out down here." Anything worth having—food, beds, that kind of thing—is down here on the main level.

"What about you?" JJ asks.

"I'll find a place to hide. See if I can figure out what they're running." Maybe my instincts are wrong. Maybe there's nothing nefarious about whoever's on this boat. But my instincts are telling me that whoever is on that boat is up to no good.

JJ opens his mouth to argue, but he closes it just as quickly. Even though our earlier fight ended in laughter, he's still being (uncharacteristically) careful, kind of tentative with me, like he's worried he might set me off again if he says the wrong thing.

JJ leads a mystified-looking Savannah back toward the stairs. I wait to hide until I see the newcomers tie off their boat, then head up the stairs. I breathe a sigh of relief when they choose the steel post farthest from the *Pogue*.

When I hear their feet on the metal stairs, almost as loud as the thunder outside, I hide in one of the closets filled with mops and brooms in the hallway leading up to the lighthouse. With any luck, I'll be able to sneak up after JJ and Savannah, tell them what I learn. I take a deep breath, smelling the bleach of the cleaning supplies in here.

At first, the new arrivals are just talking about the weather and their shitty luck getting caught in it. They don't seem to think it's strange

136

that the tower's light is on. Guess they put it down to automation like I hoped.

I make out (I think) three distinct voices. Two men and one woman. Two—one man and the woman—have accents that sound like they're from the Carolina coast; the other man has an accent that sounds more like Louisiana.

I keep listening. It sounds like the leader, the captain, I guess, is named Dax—that's the one with the Louisiana accent. I try to peek out through a gap in the closet door to see them. They have enormous, torch-like flashlights (like the one I dropped into the ocean).

"We can wait out the storm here, but I'm not missing our delivery," the one whose name is Dax says. "We're dropping this shit off first thing in the morning."

Through the crack, I can see that he's tall and lean, with short blond hair stuffed into a baseball cap. He's balancing two six-packs of beer on one of his hands, like a waiter holding a tray at a restaurant.

"Do you think they'll wait for us?" the other man asks.

"They'll wait if they know what's good for them," Dax says. "We don't want a repeat of last time."

"I don't know, Dax, that was kind of fun," the woman says, and I see her grin as she moves her hand to her waist. She taps something hidden there, and it takes me a second to realize she has a gun tucked into a holster at her side. I feel my heart start to pound.

"Fun," Dax agrees, "but not exactly as profitable as I would've liked."

The man chimes in. "Dude, the shit we're hauling this time around—they're not about to miss out on this. We're not talking about last year's iPads and iPhones anymore. This stuff is brand new." The man laughs, but Dax crosses the room and wraps his hand around the guy's throat.

"You think this is funny?" Dax asks. "Do you know what happens if we miss our delivery window?"

"I just meant," the guy says, struggling to breathe, "this stuff is valuable enough that they'll wait for it."

"And if they don't?" Dax growls. "This shit ain't so valuable if we have to toss it overboard."

That confirms it: They're pirates. Smugglers. They have some kind of contraband on their ship—electronics?—and they're due to make a delivery in the morning. Whatever their cargo is, it's so hot that if they miss their delivery time, they'd have to drop it overboard rather than risk getting caught with a boatful of stolen goods.

I guessed it as soon as I saw their ship. I don't know how I knew, exactly. It's not like the old days when pirates had a skull and crossbones flag waving from their mast. But Dad used to say that when you're on the water, you have to trust your gut, follow your intuition. Right now, my intuition is telling me to get as far from the smugglers as possible.

The one named Dax drops the other guy's neck and starts pacing from one side of the room to the other. A gust of wind rattles the tower, making the steel beams holding us above the water groan. The other man rubs his neck.

"What was that?" the woman exclaims. She reaches for her waistband again.

"Don't be a baby, Melanie. There's no one here."

"No one but the ghosts," Melanie counters.

"Ghosts?" Dax echoes.

"Yeah, didn't you know this place is haunted?"

Dax laughs. For a second, he reminds me of JJ, like he believes that if there are ghosts, he can win a fight with them. The other man crosses himself like he's in a Catholic church.

"You're not scared of ghost stories, are you, Mel?" Dax asks mockingly.

"I have a healthy respect for things I don't understand," Melanie says defensively, her hand still hovering around her waistband.

Dax opens a beer can and takes a long swig. "Never came across anything that didn't understand a bullet," he quips, then laughs at his own joke.

Shit. My mouth runs dry. What would Dax do if he found one of us here?

"Come on," Dax says, leading the way toward the bedrooms. As the three of them walk from one room to the next, their voices fade. Slowly, carefully, I open the closet door, half expecting to come face-to-face with a pirate. What if there's a fourth crew member I didn't see? But no one is there. I exhale and tiptoe up into the lighthouse.

"Pirates," I announce in a whisper when I reach the control room.

"Shit," JJ says, but Savannah looks more confused than ever.

"*Pirates?*" she echoes incredulously. "Like Captain Hook?"

JJ shakes his head, looking exasperated that Kooks are so protected from crime that they don't even know about different kinds of criminals. "Don't be stupid, Savannah."

"I'm not stupid, JJ. I just thought nowadays they were called smugglers or something, not pirates."

"It doesn't matter what you call them." JJ runs his fingers through his blond hair and paces across the control room.

JJ's family has been in the OBX for generations. We've always assumed that generations ago, his family got its start on the Carolina coast as smugglers.

"How many?" JJ asks.

"Three, I think. The captain's named Dax, plus some guy, and a woman named Melanie."

"A woman?" JJ sounds surprised.

"You think women can't be pirates?" Savannah asks irritably.

JJ rolls his eyes. "A minute ago, you didn't think pirates existed outside of *Peter Pan*." He turns back to me. "Well, three of them, three of us. At least it's a fair fight."

I shake my head. "No way. They're armed, JJ. And this guy, Dax—he's *mean*. Like, shoot first, ask questions later kind of mean."

"What are we going to do?"

"What do you mean?"

"Well, we can't hide up here all night," JJ insists. "I mean, what are the odds that at some point they won't come up here and find us?"

"What if we just explain that we were fishing on the shoals and got caught in the storm?" Savannah tries. JJ doesn't call her stupid again, but I can tell he's thinking something along those lines.

"Did you not hear John B say they're *shoot first, ask questions later* types?" JJ says.

"Savannah," I explain patiently, keeping my voice low, "they're smuggling valuable goods."

"What kind of goods?"

"Sounded like electronics, maybe. Whatever they've got, their cargo is definitely hot—stolen, I mean. They'd kill us before they'd risk us reporting them to the Coast Guard. Our lives are worth a hell of a lot less to them than whatever they're smuggling." Savannah's face goes white.

"We should've brought the spearguns up from the *Pogue*," JJ says, pressing a fist against his palm like he's gearing up for a fight.

I shake my head. "That'd be like bringing a knife to a gunfight. Literally."

"So what are we going to do?" JJ asks. For a second, he reminds me of the guys downstairs, waiting for their captain, Dax, to tell them what's next.

I gesture at the control panel. "You've had some luck with the light. We could try to get the radio up and running?"

JJ shakes his head. "Radio's completely dead. It's the first thing I tried."

I could try to get down to the *Pogue*, but her radio isn't exactly reliable when the weather's *good*, let alone in a storm like this. Savannah and JJ are still looking at me. Waiting.

"We'll think of something," I promise.

CHAPTER 20

JJ

I LOOK UP AT THE LIGHT ANXIOUSLY. I WAS SO PROUD OF myself when I got it working, but then it drew the smugglers here.

If my dad were here, he'd say I was stupid to have been proud of myself, even for a second.

I ball my hands into fists and stuff them into my pockets.

The three of us sit on the floor beneath the light. It's easier to keep still sitting down, and keeping still means that much less chance that the pirates will hear us up here.

Not that we can hear them from up here, either. The main sound is the wind howling around the lighthouse, the rain smacking the roof. I think about what Savannah said earlier, that some buildings are made to move during natural disasters. The lighthouse doesn't feel like it's moving. It feels solid still.

Unlike me. I feel itchy, like there's all this energy coursing inside me and if I don't do something I'm going to explode. It helped, after John B and I

143

argued, to kick the shit out of the controls. And then it helped, afterward, concentrating on getting the light to work.

But now, sitting still, keeping quiet—that doesn't *help*. That's whatever the opposite of helping is.

It's not because I'm angry about what John B said before. I'm not mad at him anymore. I mean, he said some shitty stuff, but we've got bigger things to worry about now.

Anyway, I was pretty much done being mad even before the pirates showed up.

I don't think I've ever stayed mad at John B.

I glance at him, trying to gauge whether he's still angry, but I can't tell.

I look at Savannah next. Is *she* mad at me? I called her stupid because she didn't understand about pirates. Maybe she hates me now.

Thinking all that just makes me need to move all over again.

Savannah and John B seem to have a much easier time sitting still than I do. They have their backs against the bottom of the light, their legs out in front of them. Savannah's ankles are crossed. John B leans his head back, the baseball cap he's been wearing all day miraculously still on his head. He toys with the ropy bracelets on his right wrist.

Me, I'm curled into a crouch, like I could spring into action at any moment.

I nearly do—jump up, I mean—when Savannah touches me suddenly.

"You were bouncing up and down," she explains in a whisper. She squeezes my leg just a little bit, then lets go.

"I was?" I thought I was keeping still. I mean, I was trying so hard to keep still.

"Sit all the way down," Savannah suggests. "It's a little bit easier that way." The look in her eyes makes me think that maybe keeping still is as hard for her as it is for me. I cross my legs beneath me, my knee bumping into hers.

"Maybe they'll leave," John B says finally.

"Maybe we can *make* them leave," I suggest.

"Yeah, but they could die on the water in this storm," Savannah protests. She reminds me of Kiara, with her strong opinions about right and wrong. Her arm grazes mine as she reaches up to tighten her ponytail.

Since when do I notice every time she touches me like that?

"Maybe someone will come looking for us." Savannah purses her lips and says, "Hunter and our friends know we're out here somewhere."

I narrow my eyes at the sound of Hunter's name. "I thought you didn't need a knight in shining armor."

"I didn't. But I think we could all use a rescue right about now."

"You think Hunter's about to ride through the storm to rescue you? He's probably sipping champagne back at the hotel, safe and sound."

"I hope he's safe and sound!" Savannah retorts. "They had to make it home through the storm, just like we did."

"We didn't," John B points out quietly.

Savannah nods solemnly. "Anyway, I meant that people know we're out here. Not just Hunter, but the others on the boat. Meghan, Alexandria, George, Dave—"

"Those are the Kookiest names I've ever heard," I cut in.

Savannah looks at me witheringly, then continues: "They're all, like, witnesses. If anything happened to us, the pirates would get caught, right?"

I shake my head. "All they really know is that we got caught in a storm. No one knows we're *here*, in the light tower. The smugglers could toss us into the ocean, set the *Pogue* adrift. No one would suspect a thing. They'd think it was just a tragic accident, a bunch of kids who didn't know any better."

I feel Savannah shiver. Maybe I should have put things more gently.

I hear Kie's voice in my head, reminding me to think before I speak.

But I was just so pissed when Savannah mentioned Hunter like that, like he's allowed to rescue her, but I'm not.

Why can't I ever hear Kiara's advice *before* I say something wrong?

"You're both right," John B says. "Somehow, we've got to get the word out that we're here. That the smugglers are here. So they'd be implicated if anything actually did happen to us."

"How?" I gesture toward the control panel. "Like I said, the radio's broken."

John B looks thoughtful, and after a second a slow smile spreads across his face.

"What?" I prompt.

"*Their* radio's not broken," he says.

CHAPTER 21

JOHN B

I STARTED OUT THINKING: *WHAT WOULD POPE DO?* 'CAUSE Pope is definitely the smartest guy I know. JJ is the best surfer (don't tell him I said so), and Kie is probably the best person I know (her moral compass points true north at all times), but Pope—Pope is the smartest. Pope is the guy you want around when you have to come up with a complicated plan.

But unfortunately, Pope's not here, so I had to come up with something on my own. (Plus, the truth is, I'm glad Pope and Kie are safe at home.)

JJ thinks my plan is off-the-wall, and that's really saying something: When JJ Maybank thinks you've gone too far, then you're really in deep shit. But what other choice do we have? Maybe my plan *is* nuts, but I figure I'm just as likely to get murdered by those pirates if they discover us in the lighthouse as I am if they discover me sneaking onto their ship to radio for help.

And if they find me—*just me*—on board, maybe they won't find Savannah and JJ up in the lighthouse. Maybe they'll believe I'm out here alone.

"I've got a better idea," JJ says before I leave the lighthouse.

"Better than sneaking onto a pirates' ship and stealing their radio?" Savannah asks sarcastically. (She doesn't think highly of my plan, either.)

"I'm not stealing it," I point out. "I'm just gonna use it."

"Oh, now I feel so much better," Savannah replies. JJ and I haven't known her that long, but she already sort of feels like an old friend. Maybe being trapped in a storm with murderous pirates below you makes people, I don't know, bond more quickly or something.

"Anyway, JJ, what's your idea?" I ask.

"The shoals are the Graveyard of the Atlantic, right?" I nod. "And you and I both know how superstitious people get on the water." I nod again. My dad told us that throughout history, sailors believed in signs and spirits and whatever else might promise them a safe crossing from one place to the next. He said it's a tradition that goes back hundreds, even thousands of years—back to the first explorers who believed they'd fall off the edge of the earth if they went too far.

"So," JJ continues, "let's scare them back out onto the water."

"What are you talking about?"

"Let's make them think this tower is haunted by the ghosts of all the people who drowned out there!" JJ is whispering to keep from being heard, but somehow he manages to make it sound like he's shouting. "Let's make ghoulish noises and flash the light and scare the shit out of them until they leave us here alone."

"And head out into the storm where *they* could die?" Savannah challenges.

"It's us or them," JJ counters. "Survival of the fittest."

"That's not what that means," Savannah points out.

JJ rolls his eyes. "Sorry, I didn't pay attention in bio class, but who cares? *We're* the good guys here, right? *They're* the bad guys."

"JJ, that's not a plan, it's an episode of *Scooby-Doo*," I say. We used to watch that cartoon together.

"That's where I got the idea," JJ admits.

In *Scooby-Doo*, the bad guy is always pretending to be some sort of supernatural creature to get his way—like scaring away unwanted visitors. At the end of every episode, Scooby and his friends rip off the villain's mask and reveal his true identity—usually just some cranky old man who complains that he'd have gotten away with his dastardly plans, if not for Scooby and the gang.

"Except we'd be the meddling kids this time," I say, laughing.

"Keep it down," Savannah breaks in. "I honestly can't tell which of your plans is worse."

"Definitely JJ's," I supply, just as JJ says, "Definitely John B's." Savannah manages a smile.

"At least with JJ's plan, we get to stick together," she says.

"Since when are you so careful?" JJ wants to know. "Who's the one who dove into the water after a giant grouper a few hours ago?"

Savannah shrugs. "That was different."

"Why?" JJ asks.

"Because that was just *my* life I was risking."

"No, it wasn't," JJ insists. "I jumped in after you, remember?"

"Well, I didn't ask you to do that, remember?" Savannah turns back to me. "And, John B, I can't ask you to risk your life like this, either."

"You're not asking me." I square my shoulders. "It's *my* plan. I'm volunteering."

"I don't like it," JJ argues.

"Let's put it to a vote," I suggest. "All in favor of JJ's *Scooby-Doo* plan?" Only JJ raises his hand. "All in favor of radioing for help?" I raise my hand. Savannah hesitates, then raises her hand, too. I grin as though I won something a whole lot better than sneaking onto a modern-day pirate ship.

JJ stops me at the top of the spiraling stairs. "You sure about this?" he whispers. "We can just hide out here if you think that's a better plan."

I shake my head. "They're all bad plans, JJ. We picked the least bad one, is all." JJ bites his lip like there's something he wants to say but can't figure out how. But I've known JJ forever, and it has been weighing on me, too.

So I say, "Hey, I'm sorry about before. You know, the shit I said. About your dad, my dad. That wasn't fair."

JJ shrugs. "It was a little bit fair," he admits. "And anyway, you never have to apologize to me. Pogues forever, right?"

I clap JJ on the back. "Pogues forever."

CHAPTER 22

JOHN B

I OPEN THE DOOR AT BASE OF THE LIGHTHOUSE AS QUIETLY AS possible. The door locks from the outside—the key is in the lock—and I lock it behind me, pocketing the key just like I told JJ I would. That way, if the smugglers hear any sounds coming from up there, they'll figure it must be the wind, since the door is locked and there's no key in sight. I tiptoe into the narrow hallway and peek into the main lobby. It's empty. I take a deep breath and turn around. Behind me, there's a door that leads onto the deck.

Outside, I crouch low on the deck as I bear-crawl past the windows that run along the first floor. The wind is howling, and the rain is coming down in sheets. The truth is, I could probably scream, and the smugglers wouldn't hear me. Then again, that much less chance that JJ might hear me shouting for help. But maybe that's a good thing, because I want him to stay safe with Savannah up in the lighthouse, whatever happens.

I don't need a flashlight to see where I'm going. The light from above is bright enough that I can see my way. Thank goodness for JJ's tech skills. The rain pours hard and fast, but my soaked baseball cap (mostly) keeps it out of my eyes. Through the windows, I see the smugglers sitting on the couches, drinking beer they must have brought up from their ship. I smile, thinking maybe I can score some drinks while I'm down there.

The winding stairs rattle beneath me as I make my way down. I hang on tight to the railings. I'm soaked and shivering. Then I cut my palm on a rusty piece of railing. Great. I grab the bandana from around my neck and wrap it around the cut.

The smugglers' ship is tied securely to the tower—so close, I barely have to jump to make it there. I take it as a good sign. Maybe this will be easy.

Now that I'm aboard, I turn on the flashlight on my phone, making my way down into the bowels of the ship. I take a turn and find myself in what must be the crew's sleeping quarters. There are three beds bolted to the walls.

I see a couple of pictures tacked up over the beds: a photo of a chocolate Lab; a poster of a band. Then I notice a picture of a couple of little kids—one boy, one girl—grinning. There's a note taped to the wall beside it: *We miss you Daddy*, it says in what must be their mom's handwriting. But there are little-kid pictures of hearts and stars scribbled around the words.

JJ said the smugglers were *the bad guys*. And yeah, they're clearly out here on the water breaking the law. But maybe they're doing it because they can't think of any other way to get money home to their families—to this little girl and little boy.

I can't help it, I think about my dad. Out there on the water time and time again. Did he think he was out there for *me*, somehow? Was he looking for something he believed would make our lives better? Didn't he know that all I wanted was for him to stick around? I wanted that more than all the money in the world. I still want it more than anything.

I see a dry, hooded sweatshirt draped over a bunk and slip it on over my dripping clothes. I wonder what it's called when you steal from a criminal. Is it, like, *less* of a crime somehow? I'm too cold to feel guilty about it.

The rooms below-deck are like a rabbit warren, one tiny room leading into another. I open one door, then another—a mechanical closet (but no radio), then a bathroom. I find my way to the galley. There are a couple of mugs with emblems on them—one for UNC Chapel Hill (who knew pirates were college educated?), another for a brand of beer. Which reminds me . . .

I open the fridge and pull out three beer cans. I stuff them into my pockets, almost laughing when I remember how JJ's shorts were so weighed down with booze that they fell right off last night. To keep that from happening to me, I put only one can in each pocket, then tuck the third into the waistband of my pants, even though the cold aluminum against my skin starts me shivering all over again.

Finally I find the control room, the radio in perfect working order. I pick up the speaker. "Mayday, Mayday," I say. "This is—" I stop myself before I say my name. Better to pretend to be Dax and say there are some kids trapped in the tower. That way if anything happens to us, the Coast Guard will know someone else saw us here: Dax, his boat, his crew. It's a strategic idea worthy of Pope!

"This is Captain Dax," I say, since I don't know his last name, "radioing from the Frying Pan Shoals light tower. We tied off for safe harbor during the storm and came across three teenagers also stranded in the storm."

I repeat my message a few times, but I don't get a response. I just have to hope that I'm getting through to some nearby(ish) ships, to the Coast Guard, to the harbor back home.

Okay. Time to get out of here.

But the rooms are like a labyrinth, and instead of finding my way back on deck, I'm facing a dead end. I turn around, trying to get my bearings. Beneath my feet, the boat rocks and bucks in the waves.

And a door right in front of me swings open.

The beer can in my waistband slips down my pants, but I barely notice the icy aluminum on my leg. Because I'm face-to-face with the scariest thing I've ever seen.

CHAPTER 23

JJ

"WE SHOULDN'T HAVE LET HIM GO DOWN THERE," SAVANNAH whispers.

"You voted for his plan!" I remind her.

"Only because *your* plan was so bad," she says.

"Don't worry," I say. "You couldn't have stopped him anyway. He made up his mind before we voted."

Savannah folds her arms across her chest. "I could've *tried* to stop him," she insists.

"Are you watching the clock?"

John B said he didn't think it would take more than twenty minutes for him to get down to the ship, radio for help, and get back to us.

"I wish we had service," Savannah moans quietly, staring at the stopwatch on her phone, one of the few features that works without cell service or Wi-Fi.

"Me, too." If John B could just text us updates, we'd know he was safe.

"There must be *something* we can do," Savannah says softly.

"We just have to wait," I say, trying to be the voice of reason, but the truth is, I feel like a tiger in a cage.

"Stop that," Savannah says suddenly.

"Stop what?"

"That tapping."

"What tapping?" I ask, then notice that I've been tapping my foot in time with the seconds on Savannah's phone.

I try to stop, I really do, but I'm too jittery to keep still. I climb back under the control panel and start fiddling with the wires to have something to do.

The light flashes.

"What are you doing?" Savannah hisses, climbing under the control panel next to me.

"Like you said, there has to be something we can do, right?"

"What if they come up here to figure out why the light is flashing?"

I shake my head. "The door that blocks the stairway to the lighthouse locks from the outside," I remind her. John B said he was going to lock us in when he left, so the smugglers wouldn't suspect there was anyone up here.

"Okay, but how is fiddling with the light going to help?"

"I don't know," I admit. "But I can't sit here doing *nothing*. Not when my best friend is out there risking his life for me."

"For *us*," Savannah corrects, and something in her voice tells me that she feels as bad as I do, being trapped up here while John B is down there, even though she barely knows him. "You know, when I woke up this morning and talked Hunter into taking me fishing, this isn't exactly how I thought the day would go."

I knew that Hunter wasn't interested in fishing! She had to convince him to take her. But then I remember I had to convince John B to take our trip, too.

"Me, either," I agree finally. I add, "Hey, I hope your friends are safe back at the hotel, like you said."

"Thanks, JJ." Savannah smiles faintly. "Me, too."

"I hope they're in the hot tub sipping champagne."

Savannah bumps my shoulder with hers. "Well, I kind of hope they're not having *that* much fun without me."

I nod, thinking about Kiara and Pope. Do they know there's a storm out here? Are they worrying about us? Or is Pope too absorbed by his homework to notice the weather, Kiara too slammed with tourists at The Wreck?

Savannah and I can't hear the smugglers below us. They might be down there singing sea chanteys for all we know. All we can hear up here is the wind howling and our own whispers.

I picture John B racing down the stairs to the boat. He could slip in the rain, fall into the ocean, and that would be that.

Savannah's right—we shouldn't have let him go down there alone.

I wasn't lying when I said that she couldn't have stopped him.

But maybe I could have.

I shake my head. John B will be fine. He knows how to handle himself. He'll be fine.

He *will*.

My hands are trembling on the wires overhead. Big John said that John B and I had to take care of each other. What would he say if he could see me now, knowing that I let his son out into the storm to take on the pirate ship alone? I take a deep breath.

"Maybe we can scare them," I say finally.

"I voted against the *Scooby-Doo* plan," Savannah points out.

"Well, I didn't. And I say we hedge our bets with both plans. If they don't believe in ghosts, they'll just think the light's on the fritz, right? And if they do, then it can only help get rid of them, right?"

I'm surprised by how much I want to hear Savannah say that I'm right, how much I want her to affirm that I can do something to help, even locked up here with her. I hold my breath, waiting for her to answer me.

Finally, Savannah says, "It's better than nothing."

My hands stop shaking, suddenly steady as a surgeon's. Wires, controls—I know how to do this.

I release the controls and the lighthouse light goes dark. I wait a beat, then turn the lamp back on, then off again. I definitely don't want it to stay dark for too long—it's lighting John B's way back up here, after all. But I want the flashes to look intentional, like a ghost is sending a message from beyond the grave.

158

"You think that's freaking them out?" Savannah asks.

"I don't know," I say, fidgeting with the controls.

Savannah stands suddenly. "I'm gonna see if I can hear them." She tiptoes toward the spiraling lighthouse stairs. The door that John B locked is at the bottom of the stairs.

"Hey, wait a second!" I hiss, but Savannah ignores me. I gaze at the controls above my head. I manage to rig them so that the light will keep flickering without me holding the wires.

I scramble out from under the control panel and follow Savannah. I move so quickly that I forget my phone and practically tumble down the stairs in the darkness. But when I reach Savannah, she's holding her phone in front of her, the narrow flashlight illuminating her face. She puts a finger to her lips. Below us, I hear someone shout, "What was that?"

"Shit," I whisper. "They heard me."

Savannah shakes her head.

"Do it again," she says.

"What?"

"Do it again," she repeats, shoving me back up the stairs.

Savannah wants me to make noise on *purpose*?

"Like you said, JJ, this door locks from the outside, and John B has the key. They'd have no way to know the door was hanging open when we found it. What will they think if they hear someone moving around up here?"

Now that someone else is suggesting my *Scooby-Doo* plan, I realize how insane an idea it was. "You seriously think those killers will jump to the conclusion that a bunch of ghosts are on the loose?"

But Savannah is already climbing up the stairs above me. She tucks her phone into her pocket, plunging us into total darkness. The next thing I know, her body smacks into mine, making me crash into the wall with a bang.

"You could get yourself killed," I whisper. I've known her less than twenty-four hours and it's not even the first time I've said exactly those words to her.

"I know," Savannah answers. "But it's better than the alternative."

Savannah grips my arm and we descend the last of the stairs, stopping at the door between the lighthouse and the rooms on the platform level where the smugglers are. I press my ear to the door and Savannah does the same thing, her face millimeters away from mine. I feel her breath on my skin.

"What the hell was that?" a woman's voice shouts.

A man says, "What's going on with the light?"

Another guy says it's probably the wind, but the woman counters with "I told you this place is haunted!"

I wait for the man to laugh, but he doesn't. Maybe we really did spook them.

But then the first man—the one with the Louisiana accent, I think John B said that was the captain, Dax—says, "Mel, I'm sure it's just the generator on the fritz. Check the lighthouse if you're so worried."

I back away from the door, but Savannah doesn't budge. After a beat, we hear footsteps coming toward the door. Someone—Mel, I guess—is jiggling the doorknob. Savannah's eyes go wide. The door suddenly seems slim and insubstantial, hardly any protection at all. I bet this is the closest Savannah's ever come to a criminal, unless you count John B and me stealing her boyfriend's champagne.

I hold my breath. Savannah reaches out silently and grabs my wrist, squeezing so tight that I can feel my pulse pounding.

"Locked," Mel announces. "Just like I thought. The only people up there are the ghosts."

"Ghosts aren't *people*, Mel," Dax says. "And anyway, it's just the generator blipping in the storm."

"The whole point of generators is that they don't blip in a storm," Mel grumbles. She knocks on the door, hard, and Savannah jumps. "Hate this bloody place," she adds. After a beat, we hear her footsteps moving away.

Savannah puts her mouth right next to my ear and whispers, "Not bad, Scooby-Doo." Her breath is warm on my cheek. She's still holding my wrist, but her grip is a little looser.

"Told ya it was the better plan."

It's dark, but I can see the white of Savannah's teeth when she smiles at me.

"Let's head back upstairs and keep the light show going."

CHAPTER 24

JJ

I'M BACK UNDER THE CONTROL PANEL MAKING THE LAMP flicker, my back curved so that I won't hit my head against the desk above. It helps to have something to concentrate on, helps to feel like I'm actually doing something to improve our situation instead of waiting up in the tower to be rescued like a princess in a fairy tale.

I guess that's what Savannah meant earlier, when she said she didn't need a knight in shining armor.

Maybe when I dove into the water after her, I took away her chance to save herself.

I have no idea what the smugglers think of what we're doing now. The way the wind is howling, I wouldn't even be able to hear if they came up here.

Worse, I have no idea where John B is, whether he's safe.

So it helps to focus on keeping the lights on.

And off.

And on again.

Savannah crawls under the panel on her hands and knees. "It's hard, isn't it?"

I shrug. Or anyway, I sort of shrug. There's not much space to move under here.

"Controlling the light is a cakewalk compared to what John B is doing."

"Is it?" Savannah asks. "You're telling me you wouldn't rather be down there?"

What is this girl, a mind reader on top of everything else? I try not to let it show, how right she is.

I don't want her to see that I'm worried.

I definitely don't want her to see that I'm scared.

"I mean," Savannah continues, "how are we supposed to sit up here while John B is down there facing god knows what?"

I think about the way she threw herself down the stairs and realize she's every bit as desperate to *do something* as I am, no matter how stupid it is—whether it's jumping into the ocean after a fish or throwing herself down the stairs. She can't handle feeling trapped or helpless.

I've never met someone who understood that feeling.

Savannah moves so that she's next to me, her left shoulder pressed tight against my right one.

"I have an idea," she whispers. Her breath is warm on my cheek.

"What?"

"Do you know Morse code? We could write *SOS* in Morse code."

"What are the chances those guys know Morse code?" I ask instead of admitting that I don't know Morse code.

"Not for them," Savannah explains. "For the Coast Guard, or whoever else might be coming to rescue us. In case John B got through to someone."

I don't like the sound of that—*in case John B got through to someone.* Like maybe even if he made it down there, even if he got to the radio safely, there might not have been anyone to hear his message.

Savannah turns off the lights on our phones to save the batteries. When the lighthouse light is on, it's plenty bright in here, but the way I have it flashing on and off, we're left in the darkness every other second.

Savannah reaches up, putting her hands over mine. "Three dots, three dashes, three dots." She manipulates the wires beneath my hands. I hadn't realized she'd been paying such close attention to what I was doing, but she knows exactly how to make the light flash. "Three dots, three dashes, three dots."

"What's that?" I whisper, feeling breathless even though we're lying still. Her fingers are still on mine.

"*SOS* in Morse code. You know, people think it stands for 'Save Our Ships' or even 'Save Our Souls,' but that's an old wives' tale. It's just a distress signal."

She continues talking, and it sounds like she's reciting a set of facts she's heard a thousand times.

"Morse code is used internationally, though it was originally created for maritime use. *SOS* was first adopted by the German government in the early 1900s."

"How do you know so much about Morse code?"

She drops her hands quickly. The light stops flickering, and I reach up quickly, guide the light back on.

"My dad taught me. When I was little, I thought it was our secret language, just the two of us." She pauses, smiles. "I had such a temper tantrum when I found out other people knew about it, too."

"So you're really close, you and your dad?" Must be nice.

"We were," she says. "He's the reason I know how to tie nautical knots and stuff. But he died when I was eleven."

"Oh," I say dumbly. I think of how she responded when I told her John B's dad was missing, the way John B snapped at her when she tried to offer comfort, the way she lingered in the lighthouse for a few moments after. Now, I know why that hurt her.

I want to tell her that John B would never have snapped like that if he'd known about her dad, but the truth is, maybe he would have. Not knowing the truth about where his dad is and why he's been gone so long has been eating at John B. I don't just mean he's worried about his dad. I think the uncertainty is changing him, making him more *desperate* somehow.

Like, the night after they wanted him to sign the papers that would make Big John officially presumed dead, John B didn't talk for, like, twenty-four hours. It was as though he knew if he talked, he'd have to consider what those papers meant. And he knew if he talked, he'd have to hear us—Kiara and Pope and me—talking about it, too.

And so he kept quiet, and we did, too.

Still, not knowing whether his dad is alive or dead has got to be better than knowing that he's dead for sure.

"I'm sorry," I say finally. "That really sucks."

I feel Savannah take a deep breath. "Anyway, he's the one who taught me to swim, to steer a boat, to fish. After he got sick, it was like every weekend was a chance for him to teach me something he knew. How to fix a car, change a flat tire."

"Don't Kooks pay people to do that kind of thing?" I ask, then immediately wish I'd kept my mouth shut. I can practically see the look on Kie's face if she heard me say something like that at a moment like this.

"We weren't Kooks back then. After my dad died, my mom married this . . . rich asshole. Everything changed—we moved to a new house on the other side of Charleston, they sent me to this fancy private school. It was like my dad died all over again. I mean, not like he died, but I mean—my whole life was different all over again."

This time I pause before I say anything, trying really hard to think of the right words. Finally, I settle on, "Guess you don't get along with your stepdad?"

Savannah's voice sounds different—lower, almost hollow—when she says, "I hate him. He's a creep."

"What do you mean?"

"He's got my mom wrapped around his finger, but I know what he's really like. You should hear the way he talks to the people who work for him. Like they're nothing. That's why he hates me. Because I see right through him."

"You really think he hates you?"

"I know he does," Savannah says.

"How do you know for sure?"

In the flash of light, I see Savannah nod firmly. "When other people are around, Wes likes to play the part of the benevolent stepdad, like I'm his personal charity case or something. Everyone thinks he's such a good, generous guy. He buys me expensive clothes, a cool car, all that kind of stuff. I wear the clothes, I drive the car, but I hate it all. Because when we're at home, every time he gets more than a couple drinks in him, he starts ranting about it. About me, I mean. He never says it straight out, but I can tell that he hates that he got stuck with me, you know? How much it sucks that his pretty little wife came with some other man's daughter. Wes just sort of says my last name over and over again when he's picking on me. *Rivera, Rivera, Rivera*, like it's a bad word or something. Or the punch line to a joke. My name. My *dad's* name."

I remember the way she introduced herself earlier, with both her first and last name. I thought she was being formal, but now I think maybe she was acknowledging her dad. Maybe she finds ways to acknowledge him every chance she gets. I bet her stepdad hates that.

I say, "Sounds like Wes is a real asshole."

Savannah's voice is cold. "He is."

"What do you do when he lays into you like that?"

Now, Savannah grins. "I start talking to my mom in Spanish. She's not fluent like I am, but she's got a few words after years of living with my dad—he emigrated from Mexico as a kid, and he wanted me to be bilingual so he raised me speaking both languages. Anyway, whenever Mom and I speak Spanish around Wes, he acts like we're making fun of him or something. As though Spanish—a language millions of people speak—is a secret code we use to talk behind his back."

"What does your mom say about the way Wes treats you?"

"She thinks it would help if I took his last name—Clark. Savannah *Clark*." Savannah wrinkles her nose like the word tastes bad. "As though I would ever give up my dad's name. As though I would ever want to be more like Wes."

"She doesn't, like . . . stand up for you?" I don't know what moms do.

Savannah laughs bitterly. "Wes has her totally brainwashed, so she picks him over me every time. You think parents always take care of their kids?"

"I thought . . ." I pause. I picture all those families we saw at the hotel last night, looking so happy, like their lives were so easy. Finally I admit, "I guess I thought *Kook* parents took good care of their kids."

Savannah shrugs. "Technically, my mom's not really a Kook—we were pretty broke before she married Wes. My dad was a mechanic."

I feel unexpectedly lighthearted. "That means you're not really a Kook, either," I say.

"Guess that makes you like me more, huh?"

"I already liked you okay."

"Yeah?" Savannah says, and in the flash of light, I can see her smiling. I feel myself blushing. I've never told a girl I liked her before, not even Kie.

Savannah says, "Can I ask you something?"

"Sure."

"What you said before, when you and John B were fighting, about your dad. Does he . . . is he—I don't know, it sounded like maybe he makes you feel as worthless as Wes makes me feel."

"He just likes to beat the shit out of me sometimes." I try to make it sound like I don't care, but there's a lump in my throat. We're quiet for a moment.

"Want me to tell you a secret?" Savannah says.

"Sure."

"I'm getting out of there."

"Where?"

"Wes's house, Charleston, the Carolinas. All of it. The entire Eastern Seaboard. I'm going away to college. My mom thinks I'm going to go to Duke—that's where Wes went—but I'm going to apply exclusively to schools on the West Coast. It's why I worked so hard not just to join the swim team but to make captain—I knew it'd look good on my applications. I'm applying for scholarships, fellowships, work-study programs—everything I can so that I'll never have to take another penny of Wes's money. I just have to maintain my GPA and keep my head down for one more year, and then I'm getting the hell out of Dodge and I'll never look back."

"Must be nice to have an escape plan," I say.

"You could have one, too," Savannah offers.

"I don't exactly get 'win a scholarship and go away to college' kind of grades." That's Pope's department. Or Kie's, with her activism.

"College isn't the only way to get out of town. You could get a job."

She makes it sound so easy. I shake my head. "I'll never leave the OBX. My family's lived there for generations."

"Yeah, but your family sucks, right?" Savannah quickly adds, "Sorry. I should've thought about how that would sound before I said it. Just 'cause I think about my family that way doesn't mean everyone else does."

"The Outer Banks is home." I can't think of any other way to explain it. The idea of living anywhere else makes my skin crawl. I never want to be away from the marsh, from the swells where I learned to surf, the shallows where Big John taught us to fish.

I add, "I'm sorry I called you stupid before, about the pirates."

"Thanks."

"I didn't mean it."

"I know."

"You're not. Stupid, I mean."

"I know that, too." Savannah smiles.

Savannah looks at me. I study her gaze in the flickering light. She drops her head so that it's resting on my shoulder. Her hair is soft against my neck. I wonder if she can hear my heart racing.

"Actually, maybe I am stupid. Even though I can't stand Wes, I still care what he thinks. Not always, but sometimes. I can't help it. Like, if my mom loves him so much, then maybe I'm wrong about him, or something."

"You're not stupid," I interrupt, but Savannah ignores me and keeps talking.

"Sometimes I think if I do something amazing—like, if I break enough school records at swim meets or get a great SAT score—he'll finally stop treating me like crap. Even though I *know* that nothing I do or say makes a difference, I still don't quite *believe* it." She sighs. "Does that make any sense?"

"It does." I swallow the sharp lump that springs into my throat.

"You want to hear something else that's stupid?"

"Tell me something else that's stupid."

"Here we were, in the middle of the ocean during a storm, with actual pirates just a flight of stairs beneath us, and I feel safer here than I do at home. No one here's going to treat me like Wes does, you know?"

"Yeah," I murmur. "I know what you mean." The difference is, I don't have to go all the way to the middle of the ocean to feel that safe. For most of my life, all I have had to do is step foot inside John B's house.

But Savannah's still talking. "Even in the middle of the ocean with those pirates downstairs. Maybe it doesn't make any sense, JJ, but I feel safe with you."

CHAPTER 25

JOHN B

IT'S A ROOM FULL OF RIFLES, SHOTGUNS, HANDGUNS, ammunition. They're stacked all around the room, some still in boxes, some loose, some on straps hanging from hooks on the walls. These guys aren't just smuggling stolen electronics.

They're running weapons.

I start to back out of the room, when I notice something perched on top of a stack of boxes just in front of me.

I freeze.

I've never seen one of these in real life before. Even the Camerons don't have one on their yacht, though Ward is constantly updating his boat with the latest technology. I've seen pictures, in the shipping catalogs addressed to Dad that still fill our mailbox and online—that's how I recognize it.

"It" is the most high-tech navigation system you can buy. It's not much bigger than a laptop computer and just as portable. I guess there are probably even more sophisticated ones that, like, the military uses, but regular people—even rich people—can't *buy* those. *This* system has thousands of maps encoded into its hard drive, and it automatically adjusts to allow for changing weather patterns in real time. It uses infrared technology to look for signs of life. Like, if you were on the water and came across another ship, this could literally scan the ship for signs of life before you boarded it. Which would be handy, I guess, for a bunch of smugglers. They could find out exactly how many people are on a ship before they board to steal its goods.

I shake my head. This kind of technology shouldn't be used to *steal*. It was designed to *save lives*. Think of all the ships that go missing across the world's oceans. If they all had equipment like this, they could stay so much safer. And if every Coast Guard rescue ship was equipped with it, think of all the people who could be rescued.

My dad told me that every year, on average, *hundreds* of ships go missing, but they don't get counted because most of them get found. But more than two dozen large ships sink or go missing forever, taking their crews along with them. It usually doesn't even make the news. And we don't even have the numbers for smaller boats that go missing, boats like the *Pogue*. Boats like the one my dad left in six months ago.

If my father had something like this on his boat, I'd be able to sleep at night, knowing how much safer he'd be.

Before I know it, I'm picking the nav system up. I just—I don't know. I could give it to my dad, when he gets home. So that next time he leaves, I won't be so worried.

And in the meantime, I could use it. Maybe. Try to *find* him somehow. Every weekend, I could use it to take the *Pogue* out. I could use Dad's maps to chart a path, dividing the water and the islands around the OBX into blocks and searching each block until I find him.

Of course, whatever I'm going to use it for, if I take this nav system, it's still *stealing*.

But I tell myself it's no different from stealing drinks from all those minibars last night or grabbing beer cans from the galley just now. Even Kiara, with her strict ethics and values, didn't feel bad about taking Kook drinks at the hotel. (Then again, she said that was because the only people who would pay for it would be either Kooks so rich they didn't notice the charge or the hotel's parent corporation, who was overcharging its guests and underpaying its workers.)

Anyhow, I know that *this* is different. This system is worth a ton of money. It'd be, like, grand larceny or whatever, right? But who knows what Dax and his crew did to get it. They probably stole it, too. Or anyway, if they bought it, they bought it with money they earned off stolen goods, right?

I shiver underneath my stolen sweatshirt. Stealing from thieves must be different from stealing from, I don't know, honorable, law-abiding citizens, right? The smugglers use this navigation system to steal from other people, or to avoid the sorts of law enforcement that might otherwise be able to sneak up on them and seize their illegal goods. But I'd be using this system to help my dad, to save someone. Just like it was designed to do.

Then again, I don't *know* for sure what the smugglers use this system for. Maybe they're just trying to stay safe on the water, too.

I wish Kie were here now, so I could ask her opinion on all this. Though come to think of it, I'm kind of relieved she isn't here. Because she'd probably point out that theft is theft, however you rationalize it, whether it's from good people or bad people. Kie would probably say there isn't really any such thing as the *good guys* or *bad guys* anyway—it's just who gets to tell the story and how they portray themselves when they tell it. Maybe the pirate with the picture of his kids over his bunk bed was just as desperate, the first time he stole something, as I am right now with the nav system in my hands.

I bet that's what Kie would say, if she were here.

But she's not.

The thoughts are whipping through my head as fast as the wind is whipping through the waves outside. One thought recedes but another is already swelling and crashing down.

JJ would say there's nothing wrong with stealing from thieves. He'd tell me that it's kill or be killed, dog eat dog. *Survival of the fittest*, like he said up in the tower. He'd tell me to take the system and get out of here as quick as I can.

But JJ didn't see the pictures hanging over their bunks. At least one of the smugglers has kids waiting at home for him, too.

Then again, these smugglers just need to deliver their goods—whatever's on this ship now—and they'll probably be able to buy another one of these. Me, I could save up for years and the cost of something like this would *still* be out of reach. If Pope were here, he'd do the math on it for me.

My decision is made. Pope can do the math when I show it to him.

Okay, but how am I going to get this thing out of here? It's pouring outside—if it gets wet, it could be ruined. And it's not like I can hold it in my arms—I kind of need my hands to get off this boat and climb the ladder back up into the light tower.

I take the remaining beer cans from my pockets and stuff the wires into my pockets instead, along with a pair of infrared glasses. I suck in my stomach and start to slide the system into my waistband. At least the metal of the nav system isn't as cold as the beer cans were.

At once, the room is flooded with light. I spin around on my heel.

Standing in the doorway, blocking my exit, is a man wearing ripped-up jeans and a black t-shirt. He's tall—taller than I am, well over six feet—and his body is ripped with muscles. His hair is dirty blond, a little bit darker than JJ's, and he smiles, revealing a gap between his bottom front teeth. Suddenly, I remember what else is in this room. Somehow, while I was focused on the nav system, I managed to (almost) forget about the walls of weapons around me. Stoically, I pull the nav system from my waistband and put it back where I found it.

He doesn't look particularly concerned that I'm here. In fact, he looks . . . amused, like some kid on his boat is nothing more than a nuisance and certainly nothing to be worried about.

He leans down slowly and picks up one of the beer cans rolling around on the floor. He opens the can with a *pop* and takes a long swig, then smiles at me again and drawls, "Looks like I've found myself a stowaway."

I recognize his voice—it's Dax, the ship's captain.

CHAPTER 26

JOHN B

I SHAKE MY HEAD. ACTUALLY, I'M SHAKING ALL OVER. I HOPE that Dax can't tell. I roll my shoulders back, trying to make myself as tall as possible (which is still shorter than he is), hoping I look older than I am. I wonder if he recognizes the sweatshirt I'm wearing. Maybe it belongs to him. Shit.

"I mean, here I was, taking my turn to check on our ship, and see what I found."

"I'm not stowing away," I say. "I was just—" I scramble, trying to come up with a cover story. "I got caught in the storm." That much is true. The words tumble out of my mouth. "I was out fishing on the shoals and got caught in the weather. I managed to make it here and saw your boat tied off. I climbed on board, hoping—"

"Hoping what?" Dax's voice is low, and he drawls the words slowly, like he has all the time in the world.

"Hoping you might be able to help me," I finish.

"Help you? Why would I help you? Looks to me like you're a scrawny little thief." As if to punctuate his point, he crushes the now-empty beer can in his hands. He's slurring his words just a little bit, and I wonder if his drawl has more to do with being drunk—they were drinking up in the tower before I came down here—than with his accent.

JJ would grab for the guns on the wall, try to fight his way out of here. But I know Dax has a gun at his waistband. And I have no idea if the guns surrounding me are loaded. Also, I don't really know how to use a gun.

I decide to try to be like Pope instead of JJ. Pope—Pope would talk his way out, using logic and reason.

I say, "I—it's just, when the ship was empty, I panicked. I thought there was no one here to help me. And when I saw this nav system, I thought—I thought I could use it to navigate the storm. I was going to bring it back to my boat and try to make my way back home. It was stupid," I add quickly, "to go out on the water by myself today. I just—I had a fight with my dad, and I needed some time alone, you know, to think. I didn't even bother checking the weather report."

Dax shakes his head. "Why should I believe you? You were just robbing me blind. Do you have any idea how much that system is worth?"

I hesitate. I don't think he'll believe me if I say no. After all, I knew enough to know what it was, what it could be used for. Finally, I try, "When I saw how empty the ship was, I thought, I don't know, maybe it had been abandoned or something."

It sounds ridiculous, and I know it. Why would they abandon their cargo once their ship was secured to the tower? Why wouldn't I have climbed up to the tower platform in search of the crew once I discovered the ship was empty?

I wonder if he can hear the way my heart is racing. In this room, in the center of the ship, I can barely hear the rain pattering down outside. Dax could kill me and no one would hear me scream. Waves rock the ship back and forth. I feel us banging into the side of the light tower.

"Where's your boat?" Dax reaches down for another can of beer. He opens it, takes a swig, wipes his mouth.

"Tied up to one of the steel poles beneath the tower," I answer honestly.

Dax shakes his head. He adjusts his stance again—he's not super steady on his feet, but he's still blocking the door completely. "The thing is, I just don't buy it. What would a nice-looking kid like yourself be doing out on the water alone, on a night like this?" Despite the accusation, Dax sounds completely relaxed, like we're two old friends catching up.

I need him to think I'm out here alone. He can't suspect that JJ and Savannah are up in the tower. "I had a fight with my dad. It was . . . bad. I needed some alone time. Thought spearfishing on the shoals was a good idea. Guess I was wrong."

"Guess so," Dax agrees, narrowing his eyes.

My story is so close to the truth that it doesn't even feel like I'm lying anymore. I did have a fight with my dad—not today, but months ago, before he left. And ever since then, I've been replaying our fight in my head.

He *has* to come home.

The last words I ever said to him *can't* be that he was a bad father.

If he were here now, Dad would know what to say to Dax to get out of here safely. Within minutes they'd be trading stories about their best and their most harrowing times on the water.

Dax shakes his head. "If you're skilled enough to make it out to the shoals to spearfish—knowledgeable enough to recognize that piece of nav equipment for what it is—then surely you know better than to head out without checking the radar." He folds his arms across his broad chest. "No," he says, "I just don't buy it. Unless there's something else you want to tell me?"

I have to tell him *something.* "I thought—I thought I could use it. The tracker, I mean. To find my dad."

"I thought you had a fight with your dad."

"I did," I insist. "But not today. It was actually a while ago. But then he left, and I haven't seen him since. I'm scared he got lost, or worse, out on the water. But I'm sorry. It was wrong to take it. I shouldn't have—I shouldn't have taken it."

Much to my surprise, Dax's face softens. "I get it, kid," he says. "You were trying to help your dad."

I breathe a sigh of relief. My pulse slows. Maybe Dax isn't all bad. I wonder which bunk was his. Maybe that picture I saw of the two little kids—maybe they're his.

"We'd all do anything for the people that we love, right?" he continues. "Even things that are morally . . . questionable." He grins. Maybe Dax hates to leave his family. Maybe he goes out on the water reluctantly, because he can't think of any other way to make enough money to give his kids a better life.

Maybe that's why my dad kept leaving.

"Anyway," I try. "I'm really sorry again. I guess I should get back to my own boat. Wait out the storm." I take a step toward the door, but Dax doesn't budge.

"Fathers and sons," he says with a sigh. "You know, my old man was a real piece of work. Nothing I ever did was good enough. Your dad like that?"

I shake my head. "Not exactly."

"What'd you fight about, before he skipped town?"

Now, Dax does step inside, leaving the doorway unblocked, but suddenly I'm not in such a rush to leave. "He didn't skip town," I say before I can stop myself, feeling defensive.

"Oh no? Then what do you call being abandoned by your dad?"

"He didn't abandon me," I counter through gritted teeth.

Dax's expression shifts again. Whatever kindness I saw vanishes completely.

"Sounds like maybe your dad left because he was tired of taking care of you. You look like you're something of a handful." Dax smiles coldly. "I can tell you from experience—sometimes a man needs a break from his kid." Dax presses one fist into his other palm. I wonder if he hits his kids back home, like JJ's dad.

Nothing like my dad.

"You don't know what you're talking about," I say, but my voice is shaking. For months now, I can't get rid of this nagging thought: What if the real reason Dad hasn't come home is because whatever it is he was chasing really is more important to him than I am? Maybe he's not missing at all; maybe he just doesn't care enough to come home to me. Otherwise, why would he leave me over and over again?

I'm breathing hard even though I'm standing still.

"I don't know, kid. Looks like I hit a nerve." Dax relaxes his posture, satisfied that his words upset me. He's still between the door and me, but he's no longer filling up the doorway.

Okay, I know my plan was to act like Pope, but talking doesn't seem to be helping me get out of what is literally the most terrifying room I've ever been in.

I have to get out of here.

I think I can make it past Dax now that he's so relaxed.

If I move fast enough.

If he's had enough to drink that his reflexes are slow.

If the boat keeps bucking around on the waves so that Dax can't steady his feet beneath him.

Basically, I can make it—*if I'm lucky.*

I take a deep breath, and I spring past him. Dax spins around in surprise. I kick my leg out, trying to knock his knee so that he'll lose his balance and fall, but instead my foot gets caught between his long legs, and when he falls, I tumble down, too. He swings his leg upwards, kicking me in the stomach. I fold into myself, the wind knocked out of me.

"Where do you think you're going, stowaway?" Dax growls.

I manage to crawl forward on all fours, trying to get through the door into the hallway. Dax grabs for my ankle, pulling me backward. I can't catch my breath. I kick my legs frantically.

Finally, I manage to speak. "I radioed for help!" I shout breathlessly. "The Coast Guard knows I'm out here; I told them you were holding us—" Shit! "*Me* hostage on the light tower."

It's not true, but Dax doesn't know that. I keep kicking. I don't look back but I can feel it when I make contact. Suddenly, Dax drops my ankle. Looking down between my legs, I see blood on his face where I kicked him.

"You broke my nose, you little shit!" he shouts, his voice muffled.

I struggle to get to my feet. My belly is tender where Dax kicked me—I stay hunched over, unable to stand up straight. I feel the infrared glasses in my pocket break as I move. My eyes widen when I remember that all the rest of the wires and attachments are still in my pockets. Maybe between the beers and the broken nose, Dax is disoriented enough that I could go back into that room and pick up the rest of the system and still make it out of here. Maybe I can still use it to find my dad.

But then Dax's hands go to his waistband.

To his gun.

Shit. He's gonna kill me now. I've got to get out of here. There's no time to waste. I start running, trying to ignore the pain around my middle.

"If anything happens to me, they'll know it was you," I shout over my shoulder. Dax is still on the floor. "They'll come looking for your ship."

I hear Dax cursing in response as I race through the galley, up the stairs, and onto the deck. It's soaking wet and the boat is bucking in the water like a wild horse. I slip and slide my way across the deck. My heart is pounding so hard it feels like my chest might explode, like maybe I'll never be able to catch my breath again. The light from the tower above is flashing on and off and off and on, but one beat stays lit long enough for me to find the ladder and leap.

The night is plunged back into darkness.

Over the wind, I think I hear Dax shouting, "You better run, kid!"

CHAPTER 27

JJ

THIS IS AS CLOSE AS I'VE EVER BEEN TO ANOTHER PERSON. I mean, it's the closest I can *remember* being. I guess when I was a baby, before she left, my mom held me in her arms. Maybe even my dad did, though that's pretty hard to imagine. And I've hooked up with girls before, and obviously I got plenty close to them.

But that kind of closeness didn't feel like *this*.

Savannah and I are wedged side by side under the control panel. There's no reason for her to still be here, next to me—I can control the wires on my own, and I don't need her to hold the flashlight—but she doesn't make a move to leave. I can still smell her shampoo—I think it's a mix of lavender and lemon, not that I'm an expert on that kind of thing. And I guess it might not be her shampoo; it could be perfume or body lotion or whatever else girls use.

Whatever it is, I'm not sure anything has ever smelled better.

I'm glad John B locked us in here. I think I could stay right here, just like this, all night.

But Savannah's got a boyfriend, Hunter—a Kook Touron who doesn't even know how to fish. The guy who *snapped* his fingers at her to get back on his boat.

"Hey, can I ask you something?"

"Sure." Savannah shifts her head on my shoulder. I feel her hair against my cheek and breathe in its intoxicating scent.

"Why are you with Hunter?"

I feel her body stiffen against mine and I know I've said the wrong thing. *Think before you speak, JJ.*

But I can't figure out why else a girl like this—smart, fearless, beautiful—would be with a creep like him.

Just as suddenly as Savannah stiffened, her body relaxes. She sighs. I feel her take one breath, another.

Finally, she says, "I know you think he's a jerk, but he's really not. He was just showing off for our friends. Trying to look tough in front of the guys, or whatever. He never talks to me like that when we're alone together."

Sounds like the opposite of her stepdad, who's nice in public and mean in private, but I manage to stop myself from saying it out loud.

Savannah continues: "It's just, I don't know . . . *easy* to be with him. His friends are my friends. We study together. My mom thinks he's so handsome and polite. Going to his football games to cheer him on gives me another reason to get out of the house every week—even if I hate football."

I don't think anything in my life has ever been easy, except maybe my friendship with John B. It sounds like something out of an old movie: the swim star and the quarterback. (Not that I know what position Hunter plays.) I imagine them holding hands in their school's hallways, getting elected homecoming king and queen, driving around town in their fancy cars or whatever Kooks do that passes for fun.

It all sounds so . . . *boring.*

"You hate football?" I ask finally.

"Oh my god, yes!" Savannah laughs quietly. "But don't tell Hunter, he doesn't know."

I scoff. It's not like Hunter's the sort of guy I'd be caught dead talking to.

Savannah continues: "I hate the way the players risk their bodies for every game. I can barely watch. It seems, I don't know, immoral that people are entertained by kids taking those kinds of risks."

She reminds me of Kiara, talking about right and wrong like that. I think how much she and Kie would like each other. Maybe when we're back home I can introduce them. Maybe they'll be friends.

But then I think maybe she hates watching because Hunter's the one whose body is at risk during football games. Maybe she's worried that her boyfriend will get hurt. Something in my belly twists, like I'm jealous.

"Now can I ask *you* something?" Savannah asks.

"Sure."

"Did you head out fishing today to get a break from your dad?"

"No," I answer quickly, without thinking like always. "It was for John B.

With everything he's got going on, he needed something to distract him from worrying, you know?"

I feel her nodding. "When my dad was sick, I joined every team at school, stuff I didn't even care about—like French Club even though I don't speak French. But French Club met every Tuesday after school, which meant one more hour when I didn't have to be at home, staring at my dad's sick face." She takes a shallow, ragged breath, and I realize that she's crying. "Now, I kick myself for every minute I didn't spend with him. I was just being a coward, staying away."

"You're not a coward," I say quickly. "You've been so brave today—on the water, with the smugglers, everything."

"That kind of brave is easy."

I shake my head. "Every kind of brave is hard. That's what makes it brave."

Savannah doesn't say anything, but at least it doesn't sound like she's crying anymore. I hope that means I said the right thing for once.

Something about her soft body breathing against mine makes me feel like I can tell her the truth.

"I told myself we were skipping town for John B, because of his dad. And because the island was overrun with Kook tourists—no offense— and I needed to get away from them, too. But the truth is, you're right—I wanted to get away from *my* dad. Not the way you needed a break from your dad," I correct quickly. "I needed a break from the way he's always hounding me."

"I know what you meant, JJ," Savannah says. "You don't have to worry about saying the wrong thing to me."

"I don't?"

"I just meant I understand what you're trying to say. Even when you called me stupid before—I knew you didn't mean it, not really."

"I'm trying to be better about thinking before I speak," I explain. "Even if I didn't mean it, it was a dick thing to say. I don't want to be—I don't want to act like a jerk." I almost say, *I don't want to be a jerk like Hunter*, but I stop myself in time.

We sit quietly for a few moments before Savannah asks, "Do you ever think about years from now, like when we're grown up and have homes and families of our own? Like, even if you stay in the Outer Banks—will we, I don't know, go back to our parents' houses for Thanksgiving and Christmas like they do in the movies?"

"I never thought about it," I answer. The truth is, I never really think far ahead the way Kiara and Pope do. Maybe I'm scared that if I do, I'll see a future that looks exactly like my dad's. Maybe I'll never move out of his house, even just to someplace down the road instead of across the country like Savannah wants. Finally I say, "Nothing in the rest of my life looks like the movies, so why should that?"

"Yeah," Savannah agrees. Then she lifts her head and turns to me, grinning. "Although, *this* kind of looks like a movie."

"What do you mean?"

The place where her head used to be feels cold. "I mean, trapped in a lighthouse in a dangerous part of the ocean, pirates beneath us, trying to scare them into leaving. The lamp flashing all eerie." Savannah gestures toward the lamp and wriggles her fingers, then drops her gaze. "The cute boy who wants to kiss you."

I press my hands to my sides.

"You think I want to kiss you?" I've never met a girl who'd come out and say it like that.

But then, I've never met anyone like Savannah.

Savannah leans back again, her face close to mine. "Don't you?" she asks.

This time, I wait a beat before answering. Finally, I say, "Do you want me to?"

Slowly, Savannah nods.

I lean forward and press my lips to hers. I put my hands in her hair, and even with my eyes closed, I can tell when the lamp goes dark. I never want to stop kissing her. Even if the smugglers burst through the door right now, even if they held up their guns and threatened to kill us—I feel like I still wouldn't want to stop kissing Savannah.

But then the door does open, and Savannah and I spring apart. I hit my head against the underside of the control panel. Savannah laces her fingers through mine, like she's bracing herself for a fight. But it's not the smugglers.

It's John B.

I wait for him to crack a joke, to point out that he was down there risking his life while Savannah and I were up here making out. Suddenly, I feel kind of guilty about it.

But John B's face stays serious. He's panting like he ran up here from below. His bandana is wrapped around his hand, and I can see some blood on his palm beneath it. His hat is gone, his hair is soaked, and he's wearing a sweatshirt I've never seen before.

"They know I'm here," he announces breathlessly.

"What?" I drop Savannah's hand to crawl out from under the panel, then reach down to help her up.

"The captain—Dax—he caught me on the ship. They had"—he pauses to catch his breath—"this amazing nav system. I tried to take it."

"You stole it?" Savannah asks.

"No," John B answers. "Dax caught me before I could." He lifts his shirt to reveal a long red mark that I know will turn into a nasty bruise tomorrow. "Knocked the wind out of me. Would've done more if he had the chance."

"What do you mean 'if he had the chance'?" I ask. "How'd you get out of there?"

John B looks sheepish. "I broke Dax's nose."

"Nice," I say, impressed, but Savannah says, "Shit." I look at her questioningly.

"When you're trapped in the middle of the ocean with a bunch of criminals, the last thing you want to do is piss off their ringleader, JJ."

"Sounds like he was already pretty pissed," I point out. "And who knows what that guy might have done if John B hadn't fought back!"

"I stole a sweatshirt, too," John B adds, gesturing to his rain-spattered hoodie.

192

"I'm pretty sure they're more pissed about the broken nose," Savannah says reasonably.

"Do they know you're up here, with us?" I ask.

John B shakes his head. "No—I was able to sneak up here without any of them seeing me. And they don't know about you guys. I told Dax I was alone. But, JJ—they're not just smuggling, like, stolen electronics. They had more weapons on their ship than I've ever seen."

"Weapons?" I echo. John B nods solemnly.

"These guys are . . ." John B pauses, like he's searching for the right word. "They're dangerous, JJ," he finishes finally. "You both have to get out of here before they have time to discover I'm not alone. You have to sneak down to the *Pogue*."

"No way. I'm not leaving you here. They'll kill you."

John B throws his hands in the air. "Better me than all three of us."

I start pacing around the small, round room. I'm not leaving my best friend to face the smugglers alone. But he's right—Savannah and my best chance is the fact that they don't know we're here.

I can't let them hurt Savannah, either.

"You gotta move fast," John B says. "It's only a matter of time before they come up here. You're sitting ducks up here."

"*We're* sitting ducks," I correct. "Why can't we all go to the *Pogue*?"

"I need to distract them so they don't notice you sneaking down there," John B insists.

"Wait," Savannah says suddenly. "Let's just think for a second."

John B and I turn to her expectantly. It's only been a minute or two since we were kissing, but it already feels like a thousand years ago.

"You think they'll kill you if they find you, right?"

John B hesitates. "I don't know. Maybe. I told them that I radioed the Coast Guard that they were holding me here. So they might think that if anything happens to me, the authorities will come looking for them. Maybe that'll be enough to keep them from hurting me."

I shake my head. "Even if that spooked them, there's still a chance they'll hurt you."

"And I never actually got through to the Coast Guard," John B adds.

"Wait," Savannah says. "Dax caught you trying to steal the nav system, right?"

"Right."

"And their boat is full of stolen"—she pauses like she can't bring herself to say *weapons*—"*cargo* to sell, right?"

"Right."

"So what if he thought you were trying to steal everything—not just the nav system, but all their cargo?"

"Savannah, what are you getting at?" I ask irritably. "We've gotta get out of here. All three of us," I add firmly. "As quickly as we can, before they find you and me and kill John B."

"Or," Savannah says, "we could make them think John B's an even bigger crook than they are."

CHAPTER 28

JOHN B

"WHAT DO YOU MEAN, MAKE THEM THINK I'M A CROOK?" I ask. Savannah and JJ are still holding hands. He catches me looking. I expect him to let go, but he holds fast.

I don't know what I was expecting to see when I got up here. I was worried the pirates might have gotten here before I did, found Savannah and JJ, and hurt them. I was worried I wouldn't make it up to the lighthouse without getting caught, but I came in the way I left—through the door directly from the platform outside into the lighthouse. On the stairs coming up, I could hear Dax shouting at the others to look for me. My hat blew off in the wind, and the rain practically blinded me.

Anyway, I definitely wasn't expecting to find JJ and Savannah wrapped around each other. Savannah and JJ had let the lamp go out, so I turned on the flashlight on my phone even though my battery was down to about twenty-five percent. It was like I was holding a spotlight on them while they made out.

JJ hooked up with plenty of out-of-town Kooks last summer—Tourons. But I don't remember him holding any of those girls' hands.

Now, Savannah lays out her plan. Unlike JJ's plan, it doesn't involve light shows or ghosts or *Scooby-Doo*. And, unlike my plan, Savannah's doesn't involve hoping that anyone else might show up and save us.

"That's the wildest plan I've ever heard," JJ says when Savannah finishes, but he doesn't sound exasperated. He sounds impressed.

"Wild enough to work?" I want to sound certain, but it comes out like a question.

Savannah's plan isn't *bad*. And there's definitely some logic to what she's suggesting. Even Pope might approve. Though he'd probably find a way to make Savannah and JJ's part less risky somehow.

"What am I supposed to do while you guys are doing your part?" I ask finally. Once again, I find myself thinking, *What would Pope do?*

"Stay hidden," Savannah says. "Stay safe. If they think they're about to lose their ship—with their cargo and their nav system on board—they'll get on board as quick as they can. We don't want them to hesitate."

"We don't want them to do a lot of things," JJ says.

"Okay, so it's not a perfect plan," Savannah admits. "But it's the best plan we've got."

"It's the *only* plan we've got," I point out. Savannah looks from me to JJ like she's hoping one of us might offer an alternate suggestion, but we don't. Savannah and JJ are holding hands again, and I notice JJ rubbing his thumb back and forth across her skin.

JJ asks, "How will we get down to their boat without them seeing us?"

I explain that at the foot of the lighthouse stairs, there's a door that leads outside, onto the platform, opposite the door that leads into the main lobby. "The door from the lobby into the lighthouse is still locked from the outside. That'll buy us some time."

"Okay," Savannah says. "But I have to admit, I don't exactly love the idea of sending anyone out into the storm like this."

I know how she feels. Even with the nav system, they could get lost, or worse. And even though Dax threatened me, there's still at least one person on that ship with a family at home. With kids who are waiting, just like I am.

"Savannah, these are *bad guys*," JJ insists. "It's us or them, kill or be killed. What choice do we have?"

I think again about good guys and bad guys, but I don't mention it. I'm already feeling anxious enough. I don't want to make it worse. But I wonder if JJ can tell how guilty I feel about sending these guys out into the storm.

I imagine Kiara's voice reminding me that Dax threatened my life down there. I imagine her voice reminding me that these guys have guns. I imagine her voice reminding me that they have the nav system. I imagine her voice telling me that people come face-to-face with bigger dangers on the water every day than these guys will face in this storm.

I take a deep breath. "This is the plan," I say. "Let's do it."

✳ ✳ ✳

JJ and Savannah leave me alone in the lighthouse. I hold my breath and picture them creeping out the door, around the platform, and down the spiraling stairs.

I wait for what feels like forever. Eventually, I tiptoe down the stairs, crouching behind the door that leads into the lobby. I wait until I hear JJ screaming obscenities from down by the boat, telling these pirates to screw themselves. Silently, I pump my fist. JJ and Savannah did their part.

"It's that kid!" Dax shouts. "He's trying to make off with our cargo! Mel, get down there and stop him!"

Shit. All three of them are supposed to go.

And they're definitely not supposed to go while Savannah and JJ are still down there. What if Mel finds them on the stairs? Savannah and JJ were supposed to find a place to hide after they loosed the ropes, but I don't think there's been enough time for that yet. Shit.

I can't stay up here—staying hidden, staying safe—like Savannah told me to. I have to help.

I know this trip was JJ's idea, and we're currently enacting the plan that Savannah came up with, but the *Pogue* is *my* boat. Being out here, on the water, is *my* responsibility.

Which makes JJ and Savannah my responsibility, too.

I'll show myself. The smugglers will see that I'm here and go after *me*, giving Savannah and JJ a chance to find a place to hide. I hope.

I don't hesitate. I fling my body against the door, hoping to break the lock. The spot where Dax kicked me hurts so much on impact that I can hardly breathe, but my body weight isn't enough to open the door.

I need more momentum. Even though it hurts, I race up the stairs and then down again, rushing headlong into the door.

"Wait! What's that?" I hear one of the pirates shout. My knees and elbows crash against the hard wood.

The door gives way, but I must knock it off its hinges entirely. Now, I'm falling to the floor right along with it.

I land hard and hear Dax's voice shout, "There he is!"

CHAPTER 29

JJ

I TOLD SAVANNAH SHE DIDN'T HAVE TO COME WITH ME. I CAN loosen the ropes myself. She could've stayed up in the lighthouse with John B or found some other hiding place and stayed concealed on the platform until the pirates were gone.

But she insisted on coming with me.

I knew she would.

When we get down to the boat, Savannah hesitates. The boat's heaving above the waves, banging against the steel post of the tower.

"What if those are their only ropes?" Her voice betrays her worry. "And the next safe harbor they find, they can't tie off?"

"They've got to have backups on board." I sound more confident than I feel, and by the look of her furrowed brow, she isn't convinced. Sending the smugglers out into the storm may be her plan, but she's okay with it only if they still have a chance of landing somewhere safe. All the better. Jumping into the boat is dangerous. If she's morally opposed to what we're doing, maybe she won't follow me.

I hold my breath and jump onto the boat, landing hard on my ankle.

When I look up, Savannah is poised to jump.

"Stay back!" I shout. I don't think she can hear me. Savannah thinks this kind of brave is easy. She leaps onto the boat before I can stop her.

"What are you doing?" I shout, furious. "We don't both have to be here."

But Savannah ignores me, getting to work on the first knot.

There are four ties: two holding the front of the boat in place, two holding the back. Savannah manages to untie the first rope at the front. The boat keeps bucking over the waves, but it's still tied securely to the tower. But when she unties the second, the boat swings out into the ocean. I see Savannah lose her balance.

"Get back on the ladder," I yell. "I'll get the other two."

"No way," Savannah says. "I'm not leaving you."

I pull her close then, kissing her in the rain, the boat rocking so wildly beneath us that I can barely make our lips meet.

"Go!" I shout, shoving her toward the back of the boat, the only part still connected to the tower. "I'll be right behind you."

Savannah leaps onto the ladder, clinging to the bottom rung with one hand. I hear her shouting as she pulls the rest of her body up. We can't use flashlights in case the smugglers look down and see us; there's only the flashing light from the tower to guide our movements.

I creep to the back of the boat and grope blindly in the dark for the remaining two ropes. I have to untie one of them completely; the other, I just have to loosen. And I have to move fast. We can't risk the pirates coming down to the boat before Savannah and I make it back up to the platform

I find the first rope. It's hard to untie it when it's soaking wet and tightly knotted. I don't know how Savannah did it. Crap. This is taking too long. Eventually, I remember my dad's Swiss Army knife, the one I swiped before we left the OBX this morning. I reach into my pocket and pull it out.

"At least Dad's useful for something," I mutter as I cut through the rope, one fiber at a time. It feels like it takes hours to cut clean through.

Finally, I stick the knife into the last rope, just enough to loosen it.

This definitely isn't part of Savannah's plan. She wanted the pirates to think their knots came undone in the storm somehow. When they see the frayed ends, they'll know someone cut the ropes.

I can only hope that by the time they notice, they'll be miles away from here. The rain is still coming down in sheets, but the wind is whipping a little less wildly, and the waves aren't quite as choppy as they were when we got here. The weather still isn't *good*—we'd never take the *Pogue* out like this—but a boat like this one should be okay.

I think.

I perch on the edge of the boat and reach my arms up, ready to jump to Savannah.

But as I leap, my ankle gives way beneath me.

I can feel the ladder rung slipping beneath my wet fingers.

I hear Savannah scream my name.

I reach out, up, searching for anything to hold on to.

I catch one of the ropes I just cut—the end still secured to the tower. I cling to it for dear life, forcing one hand over the other.

Up.

Up.

Up.

My arms hurt so much I think the weight of my body will rip them right from their sockets.

But then I feel Savannah's fingers wrapping around my wrists. Between the two of us, we pull me up onto the ladder beside her. I cling to the rungs, panting.

"You scared the shit out of me, JJ!" Savannah shouts. I don't say anything. The truth is, I scared the shit out of me, too.

Savannah and I scramble up the rickety stairs as quick as we can. We have to make a noise loud enough for the pirates to investigate and see their boat slipping away, and somehow make it to our hiding place before they see us. We crouch low on the platform. We don't turn on our phones' flashlights—can't risk the pirates seeing us. I let out a bellow, then scream until my throat is raw. It feels like all the anger and tension I've felt since we left the Outer Banks is pouring out of me. It feels good.

When I finally stop and look back at Savannah, her eyes are wide.

"Let's go," she says after a couple of seconds have passed. I grab the platform railing, following it around the perimeter of the deck, and Savannah plants her hands on my shoulders, trying to step exactly where I step.

We freeze when we see a door opening.

CHAPTER 30

JOHN B

I HIT MY HEAD WHEN I FELL. I HIT MY *EVERYTHING* WHEN I fell. I don't think I could get up to run if I wanted to. And boy, do I want to. Dax is so close that I can smell the beer on his breath.

I hear heavy footsteps coming closer. Then Dax's voice: "Looks like the kid bit off more than he could chew."

He taps my side with his boot—softly at first, then harder, right in the same spot where he kicked me before. It hurts so much it feels like my body's on fire. I gasp and my eyes flutter involuntarily, like a muscle spasm. I catch a glimpse of Dax's face covered in blood, and I swear, he's smiling. You'd think all that blood would make him look weaker—or at least, it would make me feel stronger, knowing I hurt him. But instead, he's scarier than ever.

I feel him crouching down beside me.

The other man says, "If he's up here, then who's down by the boat?"

Dax answers, "Looks like we've got more than one stowaway to deal with."

He sounds almost excited at the prospect, like kicking the shit out of a bunch of teenagers is his idea of a good time.

Silently, I beg Savannah and JJ to find a hiding place, to stay hidden, to stay safe.

The smugglers won't have time for a comprehensive search, not if they're worried about their cargo floating out to sea.

Maybe they'll be satisfied with only me.

I wonder what they'll do with me.

They might just dump my body into the ocean. Even if the Coast Guard got my message about being stranded on the tower, it might never find me. Or maybe Dax and his crew will pick me up and take me with them, like pirates in the old days, turning prisoners into workers, threatening them with a walk down the plank if they refused. Or maybe Dax won't wait that long to finish me off. Maybe he'll take out his gun and kill me right now.

Who will the Coast Guard give the paperwork to if I go missing? With my dad gone and Uncle Teddy MIA, who will have to sign the papers that say *I'm* presumed dead?

If it were up to JJ, he'd never sign. He'd hold out hope that I survived, just like me and my dad.

"Get up, you little shit," Dax barks. "Nothing fun about kicking a man when he's down."

As he says it, he kicks me again, right in that same tender spot. He laughs. Guess it's fun for him after all.

I have to get up. I have to run. I have to fight back. I have to at least *try.*

But my body won't cooperate. My eyes won't open. I feel something warm beneath my head. I think I'm bleeding.

Maybe they don't need to finish me off after all.

Maybe I'm already dying.

CHAPTER 31

JJ

WE HIDE BEHIND A PILE OF METAL CRATES AS THE WOMAN pirate—Mel—rushes down the stairs.

"She's not going to be able to secure the boat on her own," Savannah whispers. "The others will have to help her." She squeezes my shoulders, but I can't stay put in this hiding spot, waiting to hear the smuggler who went down to the boat yell to the others that they have to get on board.

I crawl across the platform until I reach the window I broke earlier. I wince as my hand lands on broken glass but manage not to shout. Carefully, I hold myself up enough that I can just barely see in the window.

I see my best friend's body crumpled in a heap on the floor.

I see a tall man—Dax, I guess—standing over him.

Kicking him.

Hurting him.

Shit.

John B was supposed to stay safe in the lighthouse! What is he doing down here?

I have to do *something.*

I don't care what Kiara would say—I don't stop, or wait, or think. I grab the nearest thing I can find—it looks like an old, rusty pulley—and throw it through the already broken window above me. I crouch back down so they can't see me, but I hear glass shattering everywhere.

"What the hell was that?" the other smuggler shouts.

"They threw something. See?" I guess Dax is holding up the pulley I threw. "You're gonna have to throw something more lethal than that!" he shouts like he knows I can hear him.

"JJ, what are you doing?" Savannah hisses. I didn't see her crawl across the platform behind me.

"Get out of here," I insist. "Hide. They're going to come out here and find me. They don't have to find you, too!"

"I'm not leaving you to face them by yourself." Savannah shakes her head. "Please, JJ," she begs. "Hide with me." She tugs on my arm. "It won't do John B any good if we make it easy for them to find us."

She has a point. I follow her back to our hiding spot across the platform.

"So much for my brilliant plan," Savannah says sadly. We don't have to worry about being overheard. The wind's louder than we are.

"Told ya *Scooby-Doo* was the way to go," I say, and she actually smiles.

The door onto the platform opens. Dax and the other smuggler rush outside, shouting. The lighthouse light keeps flickering on and off above us. I was right about one thing: The flashing light sure makes things creepy.

"Come out, come out, wherever you are!" Dax shouts.

And then, just as suddenly, Melanie rushes up the rickety stairs and sprints across the platform.

"The boat's loose!" she shouts. "We've got to go."

"Tie it off," Dax commands.

"I can't! The ropes—it looks like someone cut the ropes."

Savannah elbows me, hard, in the ribs.

"What?" Dax roars.

"I don't know what happened," Melanie yells.

"I know what happened," Dax shouts. "These little shits—"

But Melanie doesn't wait for Dax's explanation. She turns back down the stairs, clearly expecting the others to follow. The other guy does, but Dax hesitates, like he's torn between losing his boat and leaving John B—and the rest of us—behind.

"Come on!" Melanie shouts.

Dax runs across the platform. His footfalls are so heavy the whole platform shakes. He looks from one side to the other as he runs, holding a torch-like flashlight up high. I pull Savannah close and squeeze my eyes shut, like maybe there's less of a chance Dax might see us if we can't see him. We're soaking wet from the rain.

And then I hear it as he clatters down the stairs.

"Wait a minute," Savannah whispers. "Could that wild plan of ours possibly have worked?"

I lean back against the boxes behind me. I'm breathing so hard my chest hurts.

"It looks like it did," I told her, unable to disguise my grin. "Holy shit, it did."

But we're not in the clear yet. We wait a few minutes, just to be sure the smugglers are gone, then rush inside, where my best friend's body is still crumpled on the floor.

"John B!" I shout, but he doesn't move.

CHAPTER 32

JOHN B

EVERYTHING HURTS. MY NECK, MY BACK, MY KNEES, MY elbows. But nothing hurts more than my head. The pain pounds in time with my heartbeat.

I hear JJ and Savannah fighting. At first, it sounds like they're far away, but then their voices get louder and louder. I realize they're standing over me, just like Dax before I passed out.

"We've got to go for help," JJ insists.

"We can't just go into the storm," Savannah argues.

"We sent the smugglers out into the storm!" JJ counters. "If we wait for the weather to calm down, it might be too late. You stay here with John B, I'll take the *Pogue*."

"We've been over this. The smugglers had a bigger ship with a sophisticated nav system on board. You said so yourself, the *Pogue* is not equipped for weather like this!"

"But John B might need a doctor!"

"I know, but the odds are that you'll get lost in the storm before you find one."

Much to my surprise, JJ finally agrees with Savannah. "You're right. So what do we do?"

"There's not much we can do," Savannah says. "We just have to wait. Either John B will wake up, or the weather will improve."

Slowly, like my eyelids weigh about a thousand pounds, I open my eyes.

"John B!" JJ shouts. "Can you move?"

"We didn't think we should move you," Savannah explains.

I start with a small movement, wiggling my fingers, then my toes. Everything hurts, but it seems like everything still works.

"You scared the shit out of me," JJ adds.

They explain that after the smugglers left to save their ship, they rushed in but I was unconscious. They checked to make sure I was breathing, but they weren't sure if I'd broken my legs or my back or something. JJ wanted to go for help, but Savannah thought we should wait out the storm.

Carefully, I push myself up to sit.

"Take it easy," JJ warns, and I start to laugh but it hurts too much. JJ has never taken anything *easy* in his life.

"I'm okay." I stand and take a few tentative steps, concentrating on putting one foot in front of the other. "Did the smugglers really leave?" I ask.

JJ grins. "Yup. We couldn't believe it. They ran down to their ship so fast—"

"Actually, it felt like it took forever," Savannah corrects. "We were convinced they'd come back—"

"But they didn't." They're literally finishing each other's sentences like an old couple. JJ continues: "There was enough light that we could see them heading out over the waves."

"Wow." I take another careful step. "I can't believe our plan worked."

JJ shakes his head. "It didn't work. You weren't supposed to get hurt! That creep Dax knocked you out.

I nod. "I must've hit my head when I forced the lighthouse door open. I think that's why I lost consciousness—not Dax's beating." Not that Dax's kicks didn't make everything worse. I clutch my stomach protectively.

"Why were you opening the door at all?" Savannah scolds. "You were supposed to stay in the lighthouse!"

"They sent only Mel down to the boat," I explain. "They would've caught you. I had to try to buy you extra time to hide."

"It worked," Savannah concedes. "When they were leaning over your body, it gave us time to hide."

"Good." I nod carefully, like my head is made of glass.

Savannah adds, "Well, JJ threw something through the window first. But then we hid."

"JJ!" I scold. "The whole point was for me to distract them."

"You could've gotten yourself killed," JJ counters. "When I saw you lying there, I thought—"

He stops, and for a split second, I think he's going to cry. But then something in his face shifts, and instead, he's laughing. Savannah throws him an angry look—*How can you laugh when your best friend almost died?*—but after a beat, she's laughing, too. Soon, I join in.

This is without a doubt the wildest thing we've ever done, from start to finish. Going out on the ocean without checking the weather, nearly getting ourselves killed fishing, getting caught in a storm, taking shelter in an abandoned light tower, facing down pirates, playing dead, and sending them off to sea. And the worst thing that happened (so far) is I got a little banged up. Though JJ looks pretty beat up, too—his hand is bleeding, and he's walking with a limp.

"What happened to you?" I ask.

JJ shrugs. "Nothing I couldn't handle."

"We might as well get some sleep." According to my phone, it's after midnight. "If the weather cooperates, we gotta get back to the OBX tomorrow."

Savannah shakes her head. "If there's a chance you got a concussion, you shouldn't sleep, John B."

"Why not?" JJ asks.

"I don't actually know." Savannah blushes. "It's just what they always say on those medical shows on TV."

I shrug. "No problem." There's so much adrenaline coursing through me that I think I could stay awake for days.

"I'll stay awake with you," JJ offers, then turns to Savannah. "But you should get some sleep."

"I'm sticking with you guys," Savannah insists. She and JJ argue (again) and finally agree to take turns staying awake with me.

We head to the bedrooms. It's not like they were in the greatest shape when we got here, but the smugglers *trashed* them. There are spilled drinks on the floor, and the beds are unmade. Savannah wrinkles her nose. JJ finds some untouched blankets in a cabinet and leads the way up the stairs into the lighthouse. He spreads two blankets out on the floor—one for me, I guess, and one for him and Savannah to share.

"Your turn to sleep first," JJ says. For once, Savannah doesn't argue.

As JJ and Savannah curl up together, I find myself feeling a little bit jealous. Not just because JJ has a girl in his arms and I don't (though that's definitely part of it), but because JJ isn't alone, and I am.

I'm always alone.

If only I'd moved faster, I might have been able to keep that nav system. Then again, that would've meant sending Dax and his crew out into the storm without it, and I don't think I could've lived with that.

Still, I could've used it to find my dad. Then I wouldn't be alone anymore.

For the first time, it occurs to me that maybe Dad doesn't *want* to be found. He's been gone for months with no word. What if this time, he wasn't leaving on some mission, but to get away from me, like Dax said? Maybe he didn't want to be my dad anymore.

I close my eyes, just for a second. I hear him telling me stories about this very lighthouse, promising we'd go inside someday. I see my dad teaching me to fish, to drive a boat. I see him teaching me to take charge on the water. He's the reason I took action tonight, to help my friends. Because of the person he taught me to be.

He would never leave me.

Not if he could help it.

CHAPTER 33

JJ

"OPEN THOSE EYES, JOHN B," I WARN. JOHN B'S EYES BLINK open rapidly.

I'm rigging the lighthouse lamp so it'll stay on all night without flickering, hoping the brightness will help keep us awake. I slide out from under the control panel and lie down next to Savannah. I use my body to block the light as best I can—just because John B and I have to stay awake doesn't mean she shouldn't get any sleep.

"Thought you weren't tired," I tease. I adjust my body, trying to keep my ankle comfortable, but it hurts no matter what I do.

"I'm not," John B insists. "I was just . . . thinking."

I nod. I've been thinking, too. Right now, I'm thinking that nothing has ever felt as warm as Savannah's back against my front, her knees lined up against mine, her bare feet resting over mine. She sighs and her breathing shifts. She's falling asleep.

"Never thought I'd see the day," John B whispers.

"What day?" So much has happened today that he could be talking about *anything*.

"The day that JJ Maybank fell for a Kook."

I can feel my face getting hot as I blush.

John B's seen me hook up with a thousand tourists before—how can he tell this time is different? *I'm* not even sure it's different, not yet. I mean, I think it is. I think I really care about this girl. And when I hear myself defending her, I know it for sure.

"She's not a Kook," I say firmly.

"Right," John B agrees. "She's a Touron."

"No, she's not." Savannah's nothing like the girls I hooked up with last summer. "She's . . . like Kiara."

"I don't know, man." John B acts like he's thinking really hard. "Kiara may have money, but she definitely doesn't hang out with Kooks. This girl—"

"Savannah," I correct.

"Savannah's boyfriend is definitely a Kook."

I feel my face growing hot again. My whole body feels hot. "He's not her boyfriend anymore."

"Did she tell you that?"

"She didn't have to," I insist, like her kisses alone are proof that she's going to break up with Hunter.

John B rolls onto his back. "All I know is that I wouldn't be caught dead kissing a Kook."

"Bullshit, you'd kiss Kiara if you could." John B doesn't argue. "Anyway, you almost *were* caught dead tonight," I point out, and John B snickers.

Savannah shifts in my arms. "I heard that if you kiss a Kook you might actually become one. You know, like the Frog Prince." She's been awake this whole time.

"Are you calling me a frog?" I ask, pretending to be offended.

Savannah shrugs. "Ribbit."

"And I guess you think that makes you a princess, huh?"

"If the glass slipper fits."

"That's a whole other fairy tale!" I protest, but Savannah just curls up closer. "So you were just pretending to be asleep that whole time?" I ask.

"How else was I gonna find out what you guys really thought about me?" Savannah grins.

"Sneak!" I tickle her. She squirms in my arms, laughing.

Savannah may be rich, but she's not a Kook. Not really. Like I said, she's more like Kiara. She'd fit right in with the rest of us Pogues.

And John B doesn't know what he's talking about. Sure, Kiara doesn't hang out with Kooks now like Savannah does, but Kie *did* for a while there. When she went to the Kook high school, she made friends. But after a few months she learned her lesson and came back to us.

Savannah's just like that. She's only pretending to be friends with the Kooks because she got stuck going to school with them after her mom married her stepdad, but she doesn't actually *like* them or care what they think. I mean, she didn't say she was going to break up with Hunter, but she wouldn't have kissed me, she wouldn't be lying in my arms now, if she wasn't planning to. Right?

No way would this girl laughing in my arms rather be with him than with me.

No way would she rather be a Kook than a Pogue.

I stop tickling her and she settles in my arms again, kissing the tip of my nose. "You should get some sleep while you can," I say finally.

"Good night, Mister Frog," she says.

"Good night, Princess," I answer, even though I can practically feel John B rolling his eyes at us.

Whatever. He'd be just as bad if he ever fell for a girl like Savannah.

Not that there are any other girls like her.

CHAPTER 34

JOHN B

I WAKE WITH THE SUN IN THE MORNING. IN THE OBX, WE'RE far enough east that the sunrise is earlier than it is on the mainland.

For a second, in between sleeping and waking, I forget where I am. I forget everything that happened last night.

I think I'm back home. I think I hear Dad in the kitchen. He calls my name. I roll over to get out of bed and join him for breakfast.

But as soon as I move, the image of breakfast with my dad shatters. I feel like I've been hit by a bus. My arms hurt, my legs hurt, my head aches. I lift my (stolen) sweatshirt and see ugly bruises blossoming across my torso, courtesy of Dax's boots. Gently, I touch the back of my head. I think I feel dried blood, but I don't seem to be bleeding anymore.

And the sound that woke me? It wasn't Dad calling me into the kitchen, opening and closing cabinets, putting a pan on the stovetop for fried eggs. Savannah's the one saying my name.

"You weren't supposed to fall asleep," she admonishes. She turns to JJ, fast asleep beside her, and gives him a gentle smack. "And you weren't supposed to let him fall asleep."

"Huh?" JJ answers sleepily, his blond hair standing up around his face. He barely opens his eyes before he reaches for Savannah and starts kissing her.

"JJ," she insists. "You were supposed to keep John B awake." Still, she wraps her arms around him and kisses him back. Her long brown hair gets tangled up with his. I look away politely. For a second, I wonder if I'd be the one kissing her if things had gone down differently last night, but I shake the thought from my head. JJ and Savannah started bickering the moment she stepped foot on the *Pogue* yesterday. There was some serious chemistry between them from the start.

I pull off my blanket to toss at them, but my arm feels like it weighs about a thousand pounds, so I barely hit them. Still, JJ gets the message. He turns to me and grins sheepishly. I guess I can't really blame him.

"Sorry for letting you fall asleep, man," JJ says.

"Dude, you hardly slept the night before. No way were you going to make it all night."

"You should have let me stay up with him, if you were that sleep-deprived!" Savannah scolds.

"How's your head feel?" JJ asks.

"It's okay," I say. "I don't think I slept for very long. I feel fine." It's a lie. I don't feel fine. My head is pounding like the world's worst hangover.

"Promise me you'll go to the doctor when you get home," Savannah says. "Just to be safe."

"Since when are you so responsible?" JJ teases. He puts his hands on her waist and tickles her. She slaps his touch away playfully.

"Promise, John B," Savannah says seriously. "I'll be too worried about you if you don't."

JJ's right. Savannah does remind me of Kie.

"I promise," I say, but it's another lie. A doctor might ask questions—like, why didn't my uncle keep JJ and me from heading out into the shoals, and why didn't he report it to the Coast Guard when we didn't come home last night? It takes only a few bad answers before the Department of Child Services gets involved.

Suddenly, I wish we were back out on the shoals, looking for fish in the shallows. A few hours ago, all I wanted was to be safe back at home, but right now, home doesn't sound safe. It certainly doesn't sound *easy*. I don't think I've ever been as tired as I am right now. The prospect of going home, even getting into my own bed—somehow that just makes me feel *more* tired, not less. Even with storms and pirates, the truth is, there are more problems waiting for me at home than there are out here on the water.

The three of us stand and look out the lighthouse's glass windows. Beneath us, the ocean is glassy and smooth. There's no sign of last night's storm.

"It's wild how it can do that," I say. I untie the bandana that I put around the cut on my hand and trade it for a Band-Aid from a first aid kit Savannah found in the B&B downstairs, then twist my bandana back around my neck.

"Wild how who can do what?" JJ asks.

"You know, on land there are signs of a storm—knocked down power lines, uprooted trees or whatever. But out here—if you didn't know, then you wouldn't know. The ocean doesn't give anything away."

JJ raises his arms overhead and yawns. "It's too early to think that hard," he says. Savannah elbows him in the ribs, and he makes a show of being terribly wounded.

"Any sign of our pirates?" JJ asks.

I walk around the circle of the tower. There's nothing but water as far as I can see. "Guess they got away." I hope I sound more convinced than I feel. "We should get out of here, just in case, though."

"Just in case what?" JJ drapes his arm across Savannah's shoulders.

"Just in case they decide to come back, and I don't know . . ."

"Actually kill you this time?" JJ suggests. Savannah elbows him again. I grin. It's kind of handy, having her around to do that.

"How do you think the *Pogue* made it through the storm?" JJ asks.

"I don't know," I answer solemnly, hoping she's okay. Before we leave the lighthouse, I take off the sweatshirt I stole from Dax's boat and fold it neatly, leave it on the floor where we slept. It doesn't feel right to take it with me. Then I pull the key to the lighthouse door from my pocket and place it on top of the shirt. I guess the key is useless now that I knocked the door down, but it doesn't feel right to take it, either.

We head down the stairs to the platform and then down the outdoor stairs toward the water. In the sunshine, without the dark and the rain obscuring our view, I can see just how rusted these stairs are, what a miracle it is that we made it up and down so many times last night without falling through one hole or another. I'm careful on the ladder that leads down to where we tied off the *Pogue*. It's hard to imagine that our little boat made it through the night unscathed. I'm not even sure if she'll still be there. Then what the hell will we do?

And then there she is. Sitting calmly in the water like a cat in the sunshine. I squint, taking her in, then jump down onto the deck. JJ and Savannah cheer and follow me. The boat is adorned with beads of water that haven't yet dried from the rain, but other than that, there are no signs of the storm.

JJ says what I'm thinking. "Is it just me, or does the *Pogue* actually look better than she did yesterday?"

I don't answer, just walk across my boat. I lean over and check the hull. There are the same old dents and dings that have been there forever, but nothing new—no scratches from banging into the base of the tower all night.

And she's clean. No oil smudges near the engine, no soda stain on the captain's chair.

"What the hell?" I murmur softly.

"That was some serious rain," JJ offers. "Maybe it scrubbed her clean."

Okay, maybe.

It's not like she looks brand new. She's still my old beat-up boat. But still—the *Pogue*'s never looked better.

Suddenly, I'm thinking of all the ships that went down in the waters around us. I imagine all the deckhands and captains and first mates who drowned over the years. I think about how they must have taken care of their own boats and ships. I wonder if their spirits ever get restless, down in the water. If their ghostly fingers ever itch for a new boat to maintain.

I shake my head. That's ridiculous. This place isn't *haunted*, not really, no matter how many people lost their lives in these waters. There's no such thing as ghosts. Like JJ said, the heavy rain scrubbed the boat clean.

Still, I find myself looking back up at the light tower, offering it a silent thank-you. Not just for the *Pogue* but for giving us a safe place to ride out the storm. For helping us survive when the smugglers showed up. For allowing our wild plan so the smugglers would leave, and we could stay, succeed. And maybe—just maybe—for taking care of our boat, so we could head back home.

"Let's get out of here." JJ's voice breaks up my thoughts. "This place gives me the creeps."

The engine starts up easily, no hint of flooding or sputtering.

"Let's go home," I say, my hand firmly on the wheel, the *Pogue*'s deck sparkling in the sunshine.

CHAPTER 35

JJ

AS THE *POGUE* CREEPS CLOSER TO CIVILIZATION, OUR PHONES start dinging with texts and missed call alerts. (Luckily John B always keeps a solar charger on board; we take turns charging our phones.) John B and I both have endless texts from Pope and Kiara, asking where we are, if we're safe, threatening to call the Coast Guard.

There isn't a single text from my dad. I shouldn't be surprised. He doesn't notice when I'm out all night hanging at John B's, why should he have noticed this time?

"Guess we better write back before Kiara has a heart attack," John B says, interrupting my thoughts. I hope he can't tell I'm thinking about my dad.

"Guess so," I agree. John B taps out a quick text, letting our friends know we're on our way home.

"Who's Kiara again?" Savannah asks.

The sound of Savannah's voice makes all thoughts of Luke disappear and I grin. "Don't worry, Princess, she's just a friend. You'll love her."

"That's the second time you've called me *Princess*." Savannah wrinkles her nose. "Let's hope that nickname doesn't stick."

I cock an eyebrow. "Why, don't you like it, Princess? Come on, Princess, give your favorite frog a kiss. Ribbit, ribbit, ribbit." Savannah rolls her eyes good-naturedly, then settles on the bench across the bow.

If she's worried about whether some new nickname will stick, then she's definitely planning to break up with Hunter. I mean, if she was never going to see me again, it wouldn't matter what I called her.

Right?

I turn back to John B. "Anyway, you think Kie's the one whose heart would give out first? My money's on Pope. He's a walking, talking ball of stress. Do you remember the look on his face when we suggested that he skip his extra credit project to go fishing with us?"

"Yeah," John B agrees, looking out at the horizon. "Good thing he stayed home, though, right?"

"Do you think they'll even believe us when we tell them what happened?"

John B grins and shakes his head.

"Maybe we shouldn't tell them, then," I suggest, but John B says, "Nah," just like I knew he would. Pogues don't keep secrets from each other.

I glance back at Savannah. She's holding her phone gently, like it might explode in her hands. It's sunny but cold, and she's got her shoulders hunched up around her ears to keep warm. The wind whips her hair around her face, but between the strands I can see that her expression is solemn.

"Did your parents find out you were out all night?" I ask, sitting close to her, my knees knocking against hers. "Are you in trouble with your stepdad?"

I'm about to put my arm around her to try to keep her warm, when she says, "My parents think I was at the hotel all night." She doesn't offer any further explanation. She's quieter than she's been since we met, including when we were supposed to be hiding from the smugglers.

Whatever's on her phone upset her.

Once again, I don't think before I act. I reach for her phone. "Hey!" she shouts, trying to grab it back, but I hold it over my head, reading a stack of texts from Hunter.

Made it back to the island okay. Lucky that rental had a good nav system, right? Good thing we splurged on the nicer boat.

"Give me my phone, JJ," Savannah says through gritted teeth.

Shit. I shouldn't have taken the phone. Even John B is looking at me like I'm a jerk. But it's too late. I mean, I regretted taking Savannah's phone almost as soon as I grabbed it, but now I can't stop reading what Hunter wrote.

Haven't heard from you—you haven't left me for those two lowlife locals, have you? Ha ha.

I don't know what makes me angrier. That a creep like Hunter is calling *me* a lowlife, or that the idea that Savannah might like me is a joke to him.

Your mom texted me because you haven't answered her calls. I covered for you. If they ask, you fell asleep in Alexandria's room.

And finally, sometime after midnight:

Everything okay? I'm getting worried.

Savannah isn't reaching for the phone anymore. Her arms are folded across her chest.

"Took him a while to worry about you," I say finally.

"Hunter knows I can take care of myself."

My friends know I can take care of myself, too, but that didn't stop Pope and Kiara from texting John B and me all night long—so worried, about to call the Coast Guard. In my pocket, my phone dings, and I know it's them, texting how relieved they are that John B and I are okay.

Maybe I don't have the kind of dad who worries about me, but at least I have friends who do.

"Why are you defending him?" I can't help it, I'm kind of yelling. "Hunter and the rest of your so-called friends bailed on you. They left you—in the middle of a storm! Hunter left you with two strangers to take care of you."

"I don't need to be taken care of!"

"Oh, so were you going to swim back to your hotel?" Why am I being so mean? Why am I so . . . *angry* at her? A few hours ago, I was holding her in my arms, and all of a sudden I hate that I'm stuck on this tiny boat with her.

"What were they supposed to do, JJ? It wasn't safe for me to get back on the other boat. They had no choice but to leave."

"Hunter had a choice," I sneer. "Just like you have a choice when it comes to being with him."

I stop short before I add, *Princess.*

"What do you want me to do? Break up with Hunter for you? He's my *boy-friend*, JJ. I *cheated* on him. He might not want me anymore when he finds out what happened."

I hate how sad she looks when she says it. Is she really scared of losing that guy? "Good riddance, then! I thought when we got back home—"

"Home for you, JJ. Not for me. Hunter and I live in Charleston, remember?"

"I thought we'd figure something out." It's not true. I didn't *think* about it at all.

Savannah must know that, because she shakes her head.

"Okay," I admit, "it's not like I had much time to think, between hiding from pirates and keeping my best friend awake all night. But what is there to think about? You and I . . . like each other, and Hunter's a jerk."

Savannah presses her hand to her cheek, like my words literally slapped her. "I told you, JJ. He's not a jerk. He was just showing off for our friends yesterday. *I'm* the jerk. I'm the one who cheated."

I remember what she said last night, about how easy it is to be with Hunter. I guess what happened between us will make things a lot harder.

"Give me my phone, JJ." Savannah doesn't sound angry anymore, just tired. "I need to write back to him."

Before I know what I'm doing, I hold her phone over the bow of the boat, like I'm going to drop it into the ocean. "For all Hunter knows, you fell overboard last night, and your phone went right along with you."

For a second, I think Savannah's going to cry, but she stays dry-eyed. In fact, her brown eyes look at me so hard I think they might actually drill a hole right into my face. She sighs like she's daring me to drop her phone. But I'm frozen, my arm out over the side of the boat. I grip her phone tight in my hand. If the *Pogue* bucked over a wave, I might drop it.

Shit. I didn't think this through. Cue Kiara telling me that I need to think before I *move*, not just before I speak.

Hunter probably never did anything like this. Hunter probably thinks before he speaks, acts, even *breathes*. Hunter is careful, not spontaneous.

Is that what Savannah really wants?

Now that I've done this—taken her phone, read her texts, threatened to drop it into the ocean—I don't know how to get out of it.

"JJ, what are you doing?" John B calls out finally. "Give Savannah back her phone."

For some reason, when John B says it, I listen.

"Here." I hold the phone out toward Savannah. "Tell your boyfriend I say hi."

"JJ," Savannah says softly. "You know it's complicated, right? I've got a lot to figure out."

I shake my head.

It doesn't seem complicated to me.

To me, it seems like the simplest thing in the world.

CHAPTER 36

JJ

WHEN JOHN B FINALLY PULLS US UP TO THE DOCK IN THE marshes behind the Chateau, Kiara and Pope are there. I toss out the line and Pope catches it. Kiara jumps onto the boat before we're fully docked and throws her arms around me, then John B. (I think she hugs John B longer than she hugged me, but I'm not sure if John B notices.)

"We were so worried!" Kie's out of breath. "Pope saw a report about the storm on the news, and then you weren't answering any of our texts . . ." She trails off.

I hop off the boat and Pope claps me on the back. "Did you finish your homework?" I ask, and Pope shakes his head in exasperation. Not because he didn't finish his assignment—we both know he did—but because he knows—even *Pope* knows—that school isn't the most important thing in the world.

Kiara gestures at Savannah. "Who's this?"

Savannah holds out her hand to shake, but Kiara doesn't take it. Maybe she recognizes Savannah from the hotel a couple nights ago.

Kie looks suspiciously from John B to me. Savannah drops her hand, stuffs it awkwardly into her pocket.

I know I could say something. I could tell Kiara how great Savannah is—Kie would get it. And Pope never judges anyone before he gets to know them. He thinks that's not logical.

But I keep quiet. Because the thing is, I don't know how to introduce Savannah to Kie and Pope. Is she this amazing girl we met on the water, the fearless girl who'd have done anything to help us stay safe from the smugglers, the girl I fell for?

Or is she just another Kook, a girl who used us when she needed us, but will go back to her old life the minute she steps foot on dry land?

John B finally cuts in. He says, "Guys, this is Savannah Rivera. Savannah, this is Kiara and Pope."

"Hey," Savannah says, but she's looking at me, like she's wondering why John B was the one who introduced her, not me.

Then someone else is shouting Savannah's name.

"Hunter!" she calls back, and gracefully jumps off the boat.

I turn angrily to John B—how did Hunter know where to find us—and he shrugs as if to say, *She asked for my address. What was I supposed to do?*

If she'd asked me, I would've told her the wrong address to text her boyfriend so that he'd be driving around the OBX, completely lost.

But I guess that'd be a dick move, like threatening to toss her phone overboard.

I guess I'm a dick sometimes.

Unlike us, Hunter looks well rested. He's wearing clean clothes with a perfectly beat-up and faded baseball cap that he probably bought that way. (I suppress the urge to roll my eyes. Kooks, man.) He's got a fleece jacket that's unzipped, revealing a flannel button-down underneath it. Savannah runs up to him like she's expecting him to greet her with a hug, but instead, he holds up his phone.

"What did you mean, 'we have to talk'?"

My stomach twists. Guess John B's address wasn't the only thing she texted him. Maybe she *is* going to break up with him after all.

For me.

Maybe she figured out that it isn't that complicated.

"I meant—I just meant—" Savannah sounds unsure of herself. She looks at her bare feet. She left her rubber boots on the rental boat yesterday. I watch her toes curl nervously.

Finally, she says, "I wish you hadn't left me out there, I guess." She tucks her long hair behind her ears, reaches up and runs her fingers through it like a comb, trying to smooth the wild mess it became in the wind and the rain overnight.

"What was I supposed to do? Would it have been better if we *all* got caught in the storm?" Hunter sounds like he's really asking—like he's not sure he did the right thing.

"Of course not," Savannah agrees.

"Okay then, what is there for us to talk about?" He sounds nervous, not like the jerk he was yesterday. Maybe Savannah wasn't lying when she said he likes to show off in front of their friends. "Answer me, Savannah," he says. "What's going on?"

I don't care if Kiara will say I should think before I talk. Or move. Because in seconds, I'm standing beside Savannah.

"Lay off her, man." I fold my arms across my chest. "Believe me, if you had a night like the one we had—"

Hunter blinks. "I'm sorry, who are you again?"

Savannah tries to interject. "Hunter, this is JJ. He and John B kept me safe out there—"

"You wouldn't have needed them to keep you safe if you'd just stayed on our boat like you should have."

"I didn't know the weather was going to mess everything up!" Savannah insists. Her fingers are still combing her hair, getting caught in a tangle. I resist the urge to reach for her hand.

"Wait a minute," I say, my pulse pounding with fury, "do you think it's *Savannah's* fault she got caught in the storm with us? You can't blame her for the weather."

"Mind your own business, pal." Now, Hunter sounds more like the Kook jerk he was yesterday. He squares his shoulders, puffing out his chest like a bird.

"I'm not your pal." I take a step forward. Hunter's taller than I am, but I'm willing to bet he doesn't have as much experience fighting as I do. And he definitely doesn't have John B and Pope to back him up.

"JJ, stop!" Savannah intervenes. "I don't need you to defend me. Hunter's not wrong. My recklessness got me into that situation in the first place. If I'd stayed on the boat with my friends, none of this would have happened."

I step back, looking at her.

I know she feels bad for cheating, but does she wish that it hadn't happened? After everything we went through, everything we said and did last night—does she wish she'd stayed on Hunter's boat instead of finding herself on the *Pogue* with me?

Savannah's hair falls from behind her ears across her face as she says, "I should never have dived in after that fish. I don't know what I was thinking."

"Savannah," I say softly, turning my back on Hunter to face her.

It almost hurts to say her name.

I want to tell her that I don't care.

I want to tell her that if she really wants to go back to that creep, then good riddance.

But I *can't.*

"Wait a minute," Hunter says like he just figured something out. "Did you, like, *hook up* with this loser? Is that what you wanted to 'talk' about?"

Now, I don't hesitate. I spin around, pull my right arm back, and take aim.

Much to my surprise, Hunter is fast. He springs away before I can hit him and I fall forward. I scramble back to my feet, arms raised, fists tight.

"Hunter, please," Savannah begs.

"How could you, Savannah?" Hunter narrows his eyes, going from hurt to angry in a flash. "What do you think our friends will say if I tell them you cheated on me with some townie over spring break? Think any of them will take your side over mine?"

Savannah doesn't say anything, but I can tell Hunter's scaring her.

Why does she care about friends who'd reject her because she fell for someone like me? Kiara had a chance to make friends with people like that when her parents sent her to the Kook school. She got out of there as fast as she could.

Hunter's face softens. "Just tell me you're sorry and we'll forget it ever happened," Hunter offers. His voice is unsteady, like he's scared she'll say no.

"She's not going to apologize to you," I say fiercely, but Hunter ignores me.

Savannah looks at the ground. "I'm sorry," she whispers.

"What was that?" Hunter asks. "I couldn't hear you."

"I'm sorry," she repeats, louder now. For a second, I think maybe she's saying it to me, not to him. I drop my arms. They hang at my sides, but my fingers are still curled into fists.

I want to hit something so bad.

"Let's get out of this dump," Hunter says, reaching out his hand.

Savannah hesitates, then laces her fingers through his. The fingers that were laced through mine hours ago.

I'm not sure I've ever felt this angry. "Didn't your mom ever teach you not to call someone's house a dump?"

Hunter narrows his eyes. "My mom taught me to call 'em like I see 'em. What did your mom teach you? How to steal a better man's girl?"

This time, Pope and John B hold me back before I throw another punch. Hunter pulls Savannah away from us, toward his bright, shiny rented SUV, the sort of car Kie calls a gas-guzzler.

"You don't have to leave, Savannah," I try.

She looks back at me. "I told you, JJ. It's complicated."

Hunter holds open the passenger-side door for her and she climbs into the car. Hunter slams the door shut, and I flinch, like he's locked her inside. His SUV leaves a cloud of dust and dirt in its wake as he speeds away.

I have to hit *something*. I turn and punch the closest thing I can—an enormous tree in John B's backyard. I pound the bark over and over again.

It's painful, but that feels good.

"JJ!" Kie shouts. "You're going to break your hand if you keep that up."

I don't stop. I find myself wondering: Is this how my dad feels when he hits me? Is it not *me* he's actually mad at, any more than I'm mad at this poor tree—is it just that he feels like he has to hit *something* after the shitty hand he's been dealt? Is that why Savannah's stepdad is so mean to her—because he's really mad about something else, whatever it is?

I punch harder. Hitting an inanimate object and hitting your kid are not the same thing.

"Breaking your bones on that tree isn't going to make you feel any better," Pope points out reasonably.

"Come on, man, pick on someone your own size," John B says, but I don't laugh. It's not funny.

None of this is funny.

By the time Pope and John B pull me off the tree, I'm covered in sweat and my knuckles are bloody. Kiara makes me open and close my hand a few times to make sure I didn't break any bones.

"Looks like you didn't manage to do any permanent damage," she says, holding my hand gingerly in hers.

I shake my head. It sure as hell doesn't feel that way.

CHAPTER 37

JOHN B

JJ ISN'T BOXING A TREE ANYMORE, BUT HE'S NOT EXACTLY calm. He's pacing back and forth across my backyard like he's doing wind sprints and shows no signs of slowing down. Kie and Pope position themselves at either end of the yard, but nothing they say is enough to get JJ to keep still.

I make sure the *Pogue* is securely tied at the dock and turn toward my house. Dad told me that *Chateau* is French for *castle*, and that's why he nick-named our shack that. 'Cause every man's house is his castle, even if it's just an old fish shack.

I can't wait to tell Dad how JJ and I bested those smugglers last night. I'll even tell him how I had that shiny nav system in my hands.

And then I remember: Dad isn't there. He isn't *here*. He hasn't been here for months. He could be *anywhere*.

Still, some part of me must hold out hope, because when I step inside I walk from room to room—every room but Dad's office, which is still locked from the outside—like I'm making sure the house is empty. Finally, I walk back into the living room and crash onto the couch. I'm exhausted but wired somehow, like I could run a marathon or something. I suddenly understand why JJ's racing across my backyard.

After a few minutes, Kiara comes inside and plops down on the couch next to me. I untie the filthy bandana around my neck and drop it on the floor. I should take a shower, rinse away the grime and stink of the past twenty-four hours, but I stay put. My entire body aches. The fabric of the couch is itchy beneath my fingers, rough on the patches where JJ and I have spilled something or other over the years.

"JJ still going?" I ask, staring at the ceiling.

Kiara nods, pulling her legs up under her. "So . . . what happened between him and that girl—what's her name again, Georgia?"

"Savannah," I supply. I add, "I don't know, exactly, what went on between them." It's the truth. I may have walked in on them kissing and watched them cuddle all night long, but that's only part of what went on between them. I've never seen JJ act like that with anyone—he was, I don't know, *tender* somehow, at least until we were back on the *Pogue* today. Like here was this tough-as-nails girl, and for once, JJ was watching what he was saying—or at least trying to watch what he said—like he was scared that she might break if he said or did the wrong thing.

Actually, maybe he wasn't scared that she would break. Maybe he was scared she would *leave*. Not, obviously, *literally* leave. We were trapped on the tower and then stuck on the boat coming home. But I don't know, he still seemed worried that she'd find a way to leave him.

I guess he was right to be scared, since that's exactly what she did as soon as we got here.

Kie and I sit quietly for a minute. We can hear Pope and JJ arguing outside.

"Sounds like Pope is trying to get JJ to calm down," Kie says.

"Let me know how that goes," I reply, and Kie laughs. Both of us know that once JJ gets going, it's pretty much impossible to stop him. We've gotten used to waiting for him to run out of steam all on his own. He's been like that for as long as I've known him; it drove our elementary school teachers out of their minds, but he just couldn't sit still at a desk all day when we were little. And actually, it's not like he's any better at it these days.

Come to think of it, when we were kids, the only time I saw him keep (relatively) still was when we were out on the water, fishing with my dad. JJ would stand on the boat, so quiet and patient, waiting to catch something like he had all the time in the world. I mean, he still got restless sometimes—he was still, obviously, JJ—but it was still as calm as I've ever seen him. Maybe because on the water, even when you're anchored and standing still, you're really still moving, 'cause the ocean is moving beneath you.

Or maybe he needed that time with my dad every bit as much as I did. Without saying a word, Kie gets up and goes to the kitchen, returning with an ancient bag of frozen peas. I press them into the tender spot on the back of my head—Kie must've seen the dried blood—and then move the makeshift ice-pack to the spot beneath my ribs where Dax kicked me.

"You okay?" Kie asks.

I shrug. "I'll live." I can still hear JJ out back. "I wonder if that's what it's like, when Luke lays into him."

"What are you talking about?" Kiara asks. "JJ would never hit his kid."

I sit up. "Of course not. I just wonder if maybe Luke gets wound up just like JJ does."

Kie cocks her head to the side, considering my theory. Her wavy brown hair falls over her shoulders and she twists it into a bun on top of her head. "JJ isn't like Luke."

"I know that. I just meant—look, we all inherit stuff from our parents whether we want to or not. And not just stuff like whose eyes we have or the color of our hair. Like, think about how hard Pope works. He probably gets that from his dad, right?"

"Maybe," Kie agrees. "Or maybe he just understands that working hard is the only way he can get where he wants to go. Like, I didn't inherit my dad's affinity for food service, you know?"

I nod in agreement, and Kie continues: "So maybe JJ didn't inherit his temper from his dad—but maybe he got it because he's just so angry to be stuck with a man like Luke."

"Maybe," I concede.

"I guess it doesn't really matter, huh? We are who we are, wherever we got it from."

I shake my head, still thinking about inheritance. In ninth grade bio, the teacher taught us about nature versus nurture—how much of who we are is because it got passed down in our genes versus the way we were raised. And apparently, there's a lot more in our genes than scientists knew a generation ago. Like, genes can pass down more than eye color and height—they can pass down things like trauma, somehow. Like, trauma can actually *change* the genetic makeup you pass to your kids and grandkids.

"I think it does matter where we got it from," I say finally. "'Cause maybe I got my love of the ocean from my dad."

Kiara rests her head on my shoulder—one of the few places that doesn't hurt—and we sit without talking for a few moments, listening to Pope and JJ argue outside. Maybe even if Dad never took JJ and me fishing, even if he'd never taught me to drive a boat, even if I'd gone to landlocked Colorado to live with my mom—I *still* would've inherited Dad's love of being on the water. Maybe I still would've wanted to be out there on the water, and maybe he knew it, which is why he took the time to teach me everything he did. So that when I did venture out into the ocean, I'd be safe. Like teaching your kid to drive because you know he's going to steal your car.

But even with everything Dad taught me, I know things could've gone so differently last night. If we hadn't made it to the tower—if I hadn't remembered the tower to begin with—where would we have ridden out the storm?

Outside, JJ and Pope aren't fighting anymore. It's quiet.

"Guess JJ ran out of steam," Kiara says, lifting her head from my shoulder.

"It's gonna take more than an argument with Pope to calm him down this time," I say as Pope walks inside and collapses onto the couch beside us.

246

"JJ stormed off," he says.

"Where'd he go?" Kie asks.

"I tried to get him to come inside, but he said he was going home." He looks at me. "What happened out there, John B?"

"It's a long story," I answer, and neither Pope nor Kiara asks for more of an explanation. They both know I'll tell them eventually.

"We should get out of here anyway," Kie says. "Let you get some rest. You look exhausted. Anyway, I gotta get to The Wreck before the dinner rush."

"Which is just a polite way of telling you that you look awful," Pope clarifies as he stands. He claps me on the shoulder as he heads for the door, and Kie leans down and gives me a quick kiss on the cheek.

"I'll call you later," she promises.

I lean back and close my eyes, waiting for sleep to take over. If Savannah were here, would she tell me I'm still not supposed to sleep? I should've asked Pope before he left. He probably knows off the top of his head how long you're supposed to go without sleeping if you have a concussion.

If I can't sleep, I should take a shower. It's not exactly like I smell good at the moment. And I should probably clean this place up. Somehow, the Chateau looks messier now than it did when I left, even though no one's been here.

There are a million ways to die on the water. I know that because my dad taught me, but I also know that because I love the ocean, and anyone who really loves the ocean respects how dangerous it is out there. Even the most experienced sailors and sea captains come up against storms they can't survive. Even the most seasoned fisherman can be taken down by a deadly catch. Maybe that's part of why we love the ocean so much—being that close to danger reminds you you're alive.

Does my dad crave the rush that comes with being on the water? I get it. I feel that way, too, sometimes. If a swell comes in, I *have* to surf it, no matter how dangerous the conditions might be. It's like my whole body itches to get off dry land. Like, if I have to stay put, I'll explode. Like the mermaid from the fairy tale, who'll, I don't know, turn to stone or lose her voice or however the story goes, if she doesn't go back to the sea in time.

But maybe someone with that itch—with that urge for danger, that longing to be on the water—shouldn't have a kid. Maybe my dad should've found a way to stay on dry land after he had me, however bad he might have wanted to be out there. Maybe he should've remembered that every time he risked his life, he was risking my life, too.

I think about the fight we had before he left the last time. I told him he was a shitty dad for leaving me time and time again. I've been wanting to apologize ever since—a bad father doesn't take the time to teach his son to drive a boat, doesn't take his kid and his kid's best friend fishing almost every weekend. That's the sort of stuff a *good* parent does.

But just because my dad wasn't—*isn't*—a bad father doesn't mean that I didn't have a point, when we fought all those months ago.

Dad knew my mom was out of the picture and he knew that my uncle (his brother) wasn't a reliable guardian. So what did he think would happen to me, if he left one day and never came back? Kids like me don't get adopted by loving, rich families like the Camerons. Kids like me *work* for the Camerons. Kids like me end up in the system.

Didn't Dad think about that, *at all*, before he left me?

Maybe we can talk about that, and more, when he gets home.

CHAPTER 38

JJ

DAD'S PASSED OUT—OR MAYBE JUST ASLEEP, WHAT DO I KNOW?— on his bed. If he ever even noticed I was gone, he certainly doesn't notice I'm back. I go to my room and crash onto the unmade (never made) bed, but I'm not tired.

I'm not just *not* tired. I can't sit still. I pace from one side of my room to the other, kicking clothes and god knows what else out of the way to clear a path. Dad's always on my back to clean up this mess. I think there are clothes on the floor that haven't fit me since grade school. The knuckles on my right hand are bloody from boxing the tree in John B's backyard. If Pope were here, he'd tell me I should ice my hand to reduce swelling and inflammation, and Kie would spray the wounds with an antibiotic ointment that stings.

But they're not here. I left them all behind at the Chateau. Dad may be in the other room, but I'm all alone.

Hunter said he was the *better man*.

Is that what Savannah thinks?

How can she believe that? I mean, whatever happened between us, she knows that Hunter isn't anything special, right?

Guys like him are a dime a dozen on Figure 8. He may think he's better—all the Kooks think they're better than we are—but Savannah knows the truth.

Doesn't she?

But then why did she go with him this afternoon?

She said *it's complicated.* What the hell is that supposed to mean? That her friends back home would hate her if she broke up with Hunter to be with a guy like me?

Well, then what does she need friends like that for? The girl on the tower last night, that brave girl who knew Morse code—she wasn't scared of armed pirates. Why would she be afraid of her own supposed friends?

It's complicated.

There must be more to it. Maybe—maybe she started dating Hunter because he's the sort of guy her stepdad approves of. She said she can't help trying to get her stepdad to like her sometimes. Maybe she's scared that if she breaks up with Hunter, it'll piss her stepdad off. Maybe she can't be the girl she was in the tower—the *real* Savannah—when she's back home in Charleston because she's still hoping her stepdad will approve if she does everything just right. Maybe she's with Hunter because she's trying to do something right. Not, like, *really* right, but right in her stepdad's eyes—something to show him that he's wrong about her, she isn't worthless. So that he'll stop picking on her and turning her own mom against her.

Maybe she was trying to tell me that, when she said there were different kinds of brave, when she said it was complicated.

And I totally misunderstood.

And now she thinks I hate her, when maybe if I'd just said or done something different in John B's backyard, she would've stayed with me instead of leaving with him.

Shit.

✳ ✳ ✳

Somehow, this hotel looks even fancier after seeing the state of the former B&B in the shoals. Like, it's not like I didn't know this hotel was ritzy, or whatever, but it looks even nicer now that I have another hotel to compare it with.

There are still families drinking on the deck. They may be the exact same families we saw the other night for all I know. The women in their layers upon layers of knitwear—guess they finally figured out it's not sundress weather; men smoking cigars, pretending not to notice the chill in the air, because manly men like them aren't bothered by the cold. (They wouldn't have lasted a second in the March Atlantic like Savannah and me.) There are sleepy kids all cuddled up with their parents, having dinner. A group of teens in the hot tub, the closest thing you can get to a pool around here this time of year. There's the roar of the ocean in the distance, but none of the Tourons know the water nearly as well as John B and me.

Savannah's room was on the second floor. Though I guess technically it was Hunter's room, too. *Their* room. I shiver, wondering if they've made up from their fight, and if that making up led to . . . ugh. The thought of Savannah with someone else is too gross to think about. Maybe she spent the day asleep, recovering from staying up so late with us last night.

Anyway, they're sharing a room, so how am I going to talk to her? She never actually gave me her phone number—it's not like we had to text last night, we were never separated and there was no service anyway. I head for the patio doors, but tonight they're blocked by security guards.

Crap.

Okay, the second floor. That's not so hard. In fact, it's easy. I walk around the hotel, my hands stuffed in my pockets, trying to look like I'm just another Kook out for a late-night stroll. No one stops me, though I don't really think I'm fooling anyone. Kooks even *walk* differently from how us Pogues do. Something about their stride gives away that they think they're better than everyone else.

I find a drainpipe.

After the rusty ladder that led up to the tower, a drainpipe is a piece of cake. Okay, not exactly a piece of cake—my ankle is still throbbing from twisting it when I jumped on the smugglers' boat last night and my hand is aching from my run-in with the tree in John B's backyard—but still, it's easier than the ladder in the storm. The rooms all have terraces, so once I get up to the second floor, I throw my leg over a railing and land on the deck.

Easy enough.

Then I just have to hop from one terrace to the next—they're only about a foot apart and the fall down to the first floor isn't *that* far anyhow—until I find Savannah's room.

Some of the shades are closed, but most are still open. You'd think the folks inside would be admiring their ocean views, but lucky for me, no one seems to be looking out their windows. Guess it's too dark to see anything anyhow. I pass an old couple lying on their bed staring at the TV, a couple of empty rooms, a lady changing her clothes—shit, I have to duck so she doesn't see me—and then, finally, I see *her.*

Her long brown hair is parted neatly in the middle, and instead of the wavy mess it was on the water last night, it's perfectly straight and smooth. She's wearing a light blue dress with pink flowers. After seeing her in jeans and a sweatshirt, the dress looks like a costume. Despite the cool weather, she's wearing sandals on her feet.

Their room is packed—she and Hunter are throwing a party. I remember the way Hunter scoffed when Savannah asked Kiara about the best local restaurants the other night. That already seems like a zillion years ago. The rest of the girls are in dresses and sandals, too. I guess they didn't have to actually go outside to get from their hotel rooms to Savannah and Hunter's.

Savannah is smiling and laughing, but I don't believe a girl like her can really have fun cooped up in a fancy hotel room. A fancy hotel room isn't *enough* for her.

I duck as Hunter walks by the window, beer in hand. Shit. How am I going to get Savannah's attention? I drop to all fours—the window doesn't start till about waist-height, unlike the narrow glass door to the terrace, which goes all the way to the ground. I peek just over the edge, ducking every time anyone but Savannah looks my way. It takes about a dozen ducks, but finally she sees me.

She looks confused at first, but then, I swear, it looks like she's trying hard not to laugh. I can tell—she's *excited* I showed up here. And not just because it's a break from this ridiculous party.

I was right.

Savannah *was* trying to tell me something.

And now, I'm here to listen.

CHAPTER 39

JJ

"WHAT ARE YOU DOING HERE?" SAVANNAH WHISPERS AS SHE steps outside onto the balcony. She drops down to the ground next to me so that her friends inside won't see her out here with me. She's close enough that I can feel her shivering in the cold. I shrug off my sweatshirt and put it across her shoulders.

"I had to see you," I begin, even though it sounds more like a line from a cheesy old movie than anything I'd ever be caught dead saying. "I'm—" I pause and swallow. "I'm sorry about earlier. I should've listened when you tried to tell me how . . . *complicated* this all is for you."

A smile spreads slowly across Savannah's face. "You didn't have to come all the way here to apologize."

"Yes, I did," I answer firmly. "You tried to tell me, and I didn't listen. So you left thinking I was pissed at you."

"Aren't you?"

"No. I mean, yeah, I wish you'd stayed with me today, but I get it. You couldn't risk pissing him off."

"Hunter had every right to be pissed. I cheated on him."

I still hate to hear her defend that creep, but I keep myself from saying so.

Instead, I say, "I didn't mean Hunter."

Savannah blinks in confusion. "Who are you talking about?"

"Your stepdad. I mean, I know I'm not exactly the kind of guy he'd want you dating."

Savannah shakes her head. "I'm not dating Hunter because my stepdad approves of him. I told you—my stepdad doesn't approve of anything I do, no matter how hard I try."

Now, I'm the confused one. I start to stand, but Savannah grabs my wrist, pulling me back down.

"Careful," she warns. "They'll see."

"Let them see." My voice sounds different from how it did a second ago. It comes out more like a growl. "What do I care what those guys think?"

"*I* care. I promised Hunter I wouldn't tell anyone what happened."

Hunter's the one who threatened to tell their friends earlier, like he would get Savannah into trouble or something.

"Are you really scared you'll lose your friends if you dump him?" I ask.

"No." Savannah leans back against the wall, like this is all so exhausting. "I mean, yes, a little bit. Breakups are messy. Mutual friends have to pick sides."

"Maybe they'll pick *your* side," I offer, but she shakes her head.

"JJ, I'm the new kid. I've only been going to our school since my mom married my stepdad—most of these kids have known each other practically since birth. I'm an outsider."

"So, what do you need them for? People who wouldn't pick you over a creep like Hunter aren't worth knowing, right?"

"He's not a creep, JJ, I told you. I feel terrible that I cheated on him."

"Maybe you cheated on him because you're bored with him. You said so yourself—it's *easy* to be with him."

Savannah smiles. "It certainly wouldn't be easy to be with you." I'm not sure if she means because we live far apart, because I'm not friends with her friends, because of the way we bicker and argue—or something else entirely.

She takes a deep breath and speaks slowly, not quite meeting my eyes. "JJ, there's so much in my life that's so hard—my mom's checked out, my stepdad hates me, I miss my real dad like crazy. I *like* being with Hunter. I like how peaceful it is between us."

"You can't tell me you have as much fun with him as you did with me," I growl. The fearless girl on the tower can't possibly be entertained by a dull hotel-room party like the one going on inside.

"Of *course* what happened last night was thrilling." She grabs my hand and squeezes. "I felt scared and excited all at once. But this"—she gestures to the hotel room behind us—"hanging out with my friends in the safety of this beautiful hotel—that's fun, too."

"So why'd you cheat on Hunter, if he's so much fun?"

Savannah takes a deep breath. "I've been asking myself that all day. Like I said, last night was scary and exciting all at once, like when I dove into the water after that fish, you know?" I nod. "The way you made me feel—so safe, even in the middle of the ocean, even when there were smugglers with guns a staircase away—no one ever made me feel like that before. But now I'm back in the real world. Back on dry land. And I have to get my feet back under me."

Sometimes, after I've been out on the water all day, I actually find it difficult to walk when I get back home. It takes me a while to get used to the feel of solid ground beneath me. Like it takes a whole other set of muscles to work at home than it does on the water.

"JJ," Savannah continues, "I'm halfway through my junior year—I just have to make it one more year and then I'm gone. But only if I get into a good college. Only if I win every scholarship I apply for. Only if I keep breaking records at every swim meet to impress college coaches. I told you—it's my way out."

"Pope gets straight A's and he's applying for scholarships. He's going to get into whatever college he wants, and he doesn't have to hang out with a bunch of Kooks to do it."

"JJ, a bunch of Kooks is all I have! Back home in Charleston, my mom always takes my stepdad's side when we fight. It's like I lost her along with my dad, you know? I can't lose my friends, too. I can't lose the one part of my life that's easy."

I remember sneaking into the hotel a few nights ago. All those people sitting on the deck—it didn't look like they were having fun, I thought, but it did look peaceful.

Still, I can't help arguing. "I'll be your friend. John B and Kiara and Pope—we'll be your friends." We'd be better friends than a bunch of Kooks.

"I don't live here, JJ," Savannah points out calmly, clearly, like a teacher explaining addition and subtraction to a little kid. "And anyway, didn't you see the way Kiara looked at me this afternoon? She thinks I'm just another Kook princess."

I want to argue with her, but she's not wrong. After she spent a semester at the Kook school in town, Kiara dislikes Kooks more than ever, though she won't tell any of us exactly what went on while she was there.

"Well, what about your old friends? You know, at your old school—before your mom got married."

"I wasn't exactly great about staying in touch after we moved into Wes's mansion and I started my new school," Savannah explains. "Not because I didn't miss them—I did!—but because with everything going on, it just never seemed like there was time to see them, you know? I wanted to—I admit it—I wanted to fit in at my new school. I wanted to be like the kids there. So I started dressing like them, and then Hunter and I got together, and . . . my old friends will hate me just like Kiara did, for being someone else now."

"Kiara doesn't hate you. She doesn't even know you."

"You don't understand, JJ. You're free."

"Free?" I echo, almost laughing. "With Luke to go home to?"

"But you have your friends—you and John B, you'll be best friends for life. I don't have anyone who loves me like that. Who'd risk his life to keep me safe. Not since my dad died. Not even my mom."

John B didn't hesitate before sneaking down to the pirate ship last night. He wanted me to stay up in the tower, hidden and safe.

"You're not going to find someone who loves you like that, hanging out with those people," I point out.

Savannah doesn't argue, but she doesn't drop her gaze, either. She knows I'm right.

"Come on, Savannah, I know you're so much braver than this. You jumped into the water to chase a fish, you rattled the bones of a hundred-year-old lighthouse to scare away smugglers with actual guns. You can't possibly be scared to walk into your Kook school all alone. You can get into any college you want without those people." I gesture at the window above us.

"JJ, I *like* those people."

"You do?" I ask incredulously.

Savannah sighs heavily. "I told you, JJ. There's different kinds of brave. Some of them are easy and some of them are hard." Savannah's eyes are very bright.

I shake my head. "If it's easy, then it's not brave," I say firmly.

It was easy to climb up the drainpipe and hop from one terrace to the other.

It was harder to watch Savannah laughing with her friends, to wait for her to notice me.

"So I guess I didn't become a prince, huh?"

"What are you talking about?"

"You kissed me, and I stayed a frog."

Savannah shakes her head. "JJ, I don't want a prince. I told you—I don't want to be rescued. I want to save *myself*."

"You want me to believe that it wouldn't make any difference to you if I were rich—you'd still choose Hunter over me?"

"You don't go to school with Hunter and my friends. You don't even live on the same landmass that we do! It's not about money, JJ."

"The hell it isn't," I snarl. If I had money, I could visit her in Charleston every weekend. I could probably even enroll at her school, so she wouldn't have to worry about being alone.

If I were rich, she'd choose me.

"You don't know what it's like not to belong anywhere. I don't fit in with my old friends anymore. And I don't really fit in with my new ones, either."

"So you just walk around, faking a personality all day every day?"

After a beat, Savannah nods.

"How do I know you weren't *faking* with me last night?"

Savannah levels her gaze with mine. "What do you mean?"

"Like, were you just pretending, to get me to like you, so that John B and I wouldn't, you know, throw you to the pirates or leave you to make your own way in the storm?"

"How can you say that?"

"How can I not?" I retort.

"JJ," Savannah says softly, but I shake my head. Suddenly, I hate the way my name sounds coming out of her mouth.

Slowly, like it takes enormous effort, Savannah presses herself up to stand. "I better go back inside before they notice I'm gone." I start to stand, too, but she holds up her hand. "Don't. They'll see you."

I feel something inside of me harden.

"So you're saying that you meant everything you said to me last night, but you still can't be with me—can't even be *seen* with me—because it might piss off your friends?"

"No, JJ." Savannah shakes her head. "I'm saying goodbye."

She shrugs off my sweatshirt and hands it to me. I don't put it on, even though I'm shivering.

She was wearing it for only a few minutes, but I can smell her on it—the same lavender and lemon shampoo I smelled in the water yesterday, when I held her this morning.

She walks inside. I guess she'll make up some story for Hunter and his friends—the loser Pogue who's totally obsessed with her after one night together, the idiot who thought she actually cared about him.

Even though I'm cold, I toss my sweatshirt over the edge of the terrace.

I'd rather freeze than smell Savannah on me for the whole walk home.

CHAPTER 40

JOHN B

SOMETIME AFTER JJ STORMS OFF, AFTER KIE LEAVES TO BE AT

The Wreck in time for the dinner rush, Pope calls to invite me to come over

for dinner. I can hear Heyward—Pope's dad—through the phone, asking Pope

who he's talking to. I thank Pope for the invite but tell him I'm too tired to go

out. The truth is, Pope's dad doesn't exactly love me on my best day (he thinks

JJ and I are bad influences, and he's probably right), and today—unshowered,

possibly concussed, going on next to no sleep—well, I'm pretty sure Heyward

doesn't want me crashing his family dinner.

I go into my room and lie down. You'd think I'd be exhausted, but my eyes

stay wide open. So I get up and shower, the warm water soothing my sore

muscles. After I get myself clean, it occurs to me I should try to get the house

cleaned up, too. The garbage doesn't exactly smell great, the milk in the

fridge is so sour it's turning into cheese, and the piles of clothes on the floor

aren't about to wash themselves.

And maybe if I keep busy, I'll forget how alone I am.

But cleaning up reminds me that my dad is gone. None of the forgotten clothes on the floor belong to him. None of the dirty dishes in the sink came from meals that he cooked or ate. I'm throwing away moldy bread that's been in the cabinets a fraction of the time that he's been gone. I turn on all the lights, in every room (except for Dad's locked office), like that will make the house feel less empty somehow.

The lights flicker. Kie said that the storm that hit us on the shoals mostly bypassed the island, so the weather's not to blame. The lights flicker a second time, then go out completely, and the dishwasher stops running. I must've blown a fuse. I guess after months of living (mostly) in squalor, the Chateau's poor old wires didn't know what hit them when I had the vacuum cleaner, dishwasher, and washing machine all going at the same time. Plus every light on.

The fuse box is just outside the back door. I head outside and flick the fuses back and forth. A gust of wind makes the screen door slam open and shut. It's so dark, just like last night on the light tower.

Too much like last night on the light tower.

I hear something moving in the bushes alongside the house. *Shit.* Could Dax and his crew have followed me home somehow? Maybe they're here to finish me off after all.

My heart is pounding, and despite the chill in the air, the skin on the back of my neck feels slick with sweat. If my dad were here, at least it'd be more of a fair fight—the two of us against the three of them.

Three things happen all at once: a cat comes streaking out from behind the bushes, the lights in the Chateau turn back on, and my phone—which I left on the kitchen table inside—starts ringing.

I jump as the cat streaks past, bending forward to put my hands on my knees to catch my breath. I don't think I've ever been so scared, not even last night on the water. I'm shaking from head to foot.

Slowly, I stand up straight, willing my heart to resume a normal beat instead of racing a mile a minute.

It was just a cat, I tell myself.

Just a blown fuse.

Just the phone ringing.

I grab the phone just before it goes to voicemail.

"Hey, Kie," I say breathlessly. I notice that it's after ten; her shift at The Wreck just ended.

"You'll never believe how much I made in tips tonight," she says instead of hello.

"Good for you," I answer. I lock the back door—something I never do—and collapse onto the couch.

"What's wrong?" Kie asks suddenly.

"What? Nothing."

"Your voice sounds weird."

I shake my head. "I'm just out of breath because I was running around cleaning."

"Cleaning?" Kie echoes. "During spring break at eleven o'clock at night? You sure the real John B came back from the shoals today?"

With Ki'es voice in my ear, my heartbeat resumes a normal pace. I sit on the couch. "It's me," I promise. "I just didn't have anything else to do."

Kie knows better than to ask what I mean by that, or to cluck over me like a mother hen. Instead, she launches into stories about the Kooks and Tourons she served tonight—the kids who wouldn't stop screaming, the big tippers and the cheapskates, the teens who tried to fool her dad with a fake ID, and the well-over-age people who got way too drunk. She talks almost nonstop. I put my phone on speaker, and her voice fills the room.

Then another sound joins in. JJ's banging on the back door. I get up and let him inside.

"Why'd you lock the door?" JJ asks, blinking in the bright light. I shrug. I don't want to admit that I mistook a cat for Dax.

JJ's only wearing a t-shirt with his jeans, and he's shivering. He heads straight to the kitchen and pulls a can of beer from the fridge like this is his place as much as mine, the same way he always has (though when we were little, it was juice boxes instead of beer cans). He sits heavily on the couch next to me.

"Hey, JJ," Kie says through the phone. JJ nods in response like Kie can see him. Kie says, "I'll let you go now. Sounds like maybe you've got your hands full."

"Yeah," I agree. "Hey, Kie—thanks."

She doesn't ask what for, so I don't have to tell her how much it helped to have my empty house full of her voice. How much it meant that she understood I was in no mood to talk but didn't push me about why.

"Any time." Kie answers. "Oh, I almost forgot," she adds. "You guys should come have lunch at The Wreck tomorrow. It's so crowded my dad won't notice if I sneak you some stuff on the house."

"That sounds awesome," I say. "I'm hungry already."

I turn and see JJ on the couch beside me, staring into space. JJ, whose bright idea it was to go to the shoals in the first place. JJ, who's been showing up at this house uninvited and unannounced for as long as he can remember. JJ, who seems more at home here than he ever has in his actual home.

I always thought JJ came here because he hated being at home. And sure, that's definitely part of it. But now I think maybe, since my dad's been gone, JJ's always showing up because he doesn't want me to be alone.

And I realize that I'm grateful to have him here.

CHAPTER 41

JJ

I CRASH AT JOHN B'S, THOUGH MAYBE YOU CAN'T CALL A mostly sleepless night crashing. After so many hours on the water, my body still feels like it's rocking on the boat, even lying still on John B's couch.

When I finally fall asleep, I dream that I'm in the water. It's summertime and the sun is shining and I'm floating on my back. Someone is floating beside me, holding my hand. I know without looking that it's Savannah. Guess my subconscious isn't as angry at her as the rest of me.

So now I'm angry at my subconscious, too.

* * *

By the time I wake up, it's after noon and John B is dragging me to The Wreck for lunch. We can't usually afford to eat there, but Kie promises that with the spring break crowds she'll be able to sneak us some food, *gratis*.

"What's *gratis*?" I mumble sleepily as we walk into the restaurant.

I'm still wearing the clothes I wore to Savannah's hotel last night: beat-up jeans, sneakers with no socks. John B lent me a windbreaker to wear over my t-shirt.

"It means 'on the house,'" Kiara answers, balancing a tray on her shoulder. "Just grab a table wherever you can."

Inside, the restaurant is packed. It's barely 50 degrees today and cloudy, so the tables and chairs on the deck outside—packed solid in the summertime—are mostly empty. Kie's dad never set up heating lamps like they have at the hotel.

I'd rather be cold than stuck in a crowd today, so I lead the way through the restaurant and out to the deck. John B follows; in a few minutes, Pope joins us.

"Why're we sitting out here?" Pope asks, rubbing his hands together.

"You don't know cold till you're submerged in the Atlantic in March." I try to sound wise, but I really just sound tired. Still, I add, "Maybe the cold will never bother me again. You know, maybe I've built up a whole new tolerance."

Pope shakes his head. "That's not how body temperature works," he says, but I don't listen as he launches into a scientific explanation.

The truth is, I'm freezing. I want to sit on my hands, stuff them into my pockets, but I don't want John B or Pope to know I'm uncomfortable.

When I showed up at his place last night, John B didn't ask where I'd been or why I was only wearing a t-shirt. Guess my reasons were written on my face.

"She's just as bad as the rest of them," I said after he got off the phone with Kie.

I thought Savannah was like Kiara—that even though she was technically a Kook, she had no interest in the Kook lifestyle, but I was wrong. She's nothing like Kiara. She actually *likes* her Kook friends, her Kook boyfriend.

How could anyone like Kooks *and* like me? There's no way. The two things are mutually exclusive.

Which means Savannah must've been lying all along. Last night, I told John B, "She was playing us the whole time, 'cause she needed our help to make it through the night."

"You really think so?" John B asked.

"I really do," I said, that harsh growl still stuck in my throat.

She never cared.

She never liked me.

I imagine Savannah partying in her and Hunter's hotel room, laughing with her crappy friends. Maybe she was lying about her stepdad, too, to get me to feel sorry for her so I'd, I don't know, protect her from the pirates that much more. Probably she adores the guy.

I bet she loves the car he bought her to drive around town, and I bet he gave her her own platinum credit card—or whatever rich kids have—so she could shop for clothes as much as she wants.

She probably barely even misses her dad. Maybe she's glad he's gone, because if he hadn't died, her mother wouldn't have remarried, and she wouldn't be rich.

Or maybe she was lying about her dad, too. Maybe he's not even dead!

271

Maybe she's been rich her whole life. She doesn't have old friends or new friends—she was just lying to get me away from the hotel last night without making a scene.

Well, any more of a scene than I already did.

After I left, maybe she and her friends laughed at me, the Pogue who fell for her tricks. Maybe Hunter was in on it, too, just pretending to be pissed off that she hooked up with me. Maybe they do this sort of thing all the time, playing some sort of weird power trip game with unsuspecting locals every time they go on vacation.

"And on top of everything else, she stole your sweatshirt," John B said, throwing me a blanket. I didn't tell him that I left it behind. I didn't want to talk about it.

I don't think I'll ever want to talk about it.

Now, Kiara carries a tray laden with clam chowder to our table.

"What are you guys doing out here?" she asks, though the weather doesn't seem to bother her. I guess she's warm from rushing from one table to the next.

"JJ's developed a new tolerance for the cold," Pope explains.

"Then I guess you can give me back my windbreaker," John B says, reaching across the table to undo the zipper.

"Hey!" I shout, standing up quickly and backing away. My chair lands on the deck with a clatter. I spill chowder all over John B's jacket.

"JJ!" Kie whisper-shouts. "You're gonna get me in trouble! My dad doesn't exactly know I'm sneaking you guys free food."

Kie bends down to pick up my chair, but she's smiling. Unlike Savannah, Kie's not embarrassed by me. She knows that the Kooks are the real embarrassment.

John B tosses me some napkins. I try to wipe the chowder away, but do a bad job on purpose.

"Sorry, man," I say to John B, "I think your jacket's gonna smell like clams forever."

Kie faux gags. After working at this restaurant half her life, she knows exactly how days-old clams stink better than any of us. John B throws more napkins at me, but I dodge them.

"At least there's no one else out here to notice what a mess you are," John B says, but almost as soon as the words leave his mouth, a long, skinny table next to ours fills up. It's a group of teen Kooks, bundled up against the cold.

"Gotta go," Kie says. "Tourons to please." She holds up her hand and rubs her fingers together, like at least she'll get a big tip from such a large group.

One of the Tourons pulls out a wireless speaker and turns on some terrible music at a deafening volume. Pope says, "I thought our local Kooks were bad, but these out-of-towners might be worse."

"Tell me about it," I say.

I see Hunter before I see her. He's the kind of guy who walks into every room like he owns the place, his shoulders thrown back, his arms swinging at his sides like clubs. I squeeze my spoon, which makes me wince. The scrapes on my right hand have scabbed over, but my knuckles are still tender and sore.

And then there she is, a few steps behind. She's got on another dress, just like the first time I saw her and like last night, too, even though there's nothing fancy about Kie's restaurant. She's wearing a denim jacket with a scarf wrapped around her neck.

Her long hair is pulled into a tight ponytail, perfectly smooth and straight, not one strand out of place. She's wearing makeup like she was the first time I saw her—unlike our night on the water—dark eyeliner and bright, glossy lipstick.

I drop my gaze so she won't see me staring, but then I change my mind. I may be broke and covered in clam chowder, but I have nothing to be embarrassed about.

She's the one who should be ashamed.

I was wrong: Savannah isn't just as bad as the rest of them. She's *worse*.

She's worse because she had a choice.

If she was telling the truth and she used to be poor, and her dad died, and all that—then she had a choice, and she still chose the Kooks.

She still chose people who would reject her for liking me, while I'm sitting with three people who would never reject me just because I fell for a Kook.

Three people who would never reject me, period.

Not that I'll ever make that mistake again—falling for a Kook, I mean. None of us Pogues will make *that* mistake. Kiara knows better, after the time she spent at the Kook school. Pope hardly looks up from his books enough to notice girls anyway. (At least, that's what he acts like.) And John B saw up close what Savannah did to me, so he definitely knows better.

Kooks can't be trusted. I always knew it, I guess, but now I'm even more sure.

So I look Savannah in the eye while she pretends to laugh at something Hunter said. When she sees me, her smile drops, and she looks really and truly sad. But I don't feel sorry for her.

Maybe it was all an act, maybe it was real. It doesn't matter. Wherever she came from, whatever the truth about her is—she's a Kook now.

Looking at my friends, I know Savannah's wrong that there's only one way for her to get out of town. Kie and Pope have big plans, and they know they don't have to hang with Kooks to achieve them.

And Savannah's wrong about something else, too. When we were alone in the lighthouse, she asked me why I didn't want to leave the Outer Banks. Why would I want to stay, she said, when my family sucks?

And yeah, maybe my dad does suck. But my dad isn't the only family I have.

Savannah may need to run away from home to find her people, but I don't.

I have the Pogues, right here, right now.

CHAPTER 42

JOHN B

KIE BRINGS OVER FOUR PLASTIC CUPS. "HERE ARE THE SODAS you ordered," she says with a flourish. She's wearing tight jeans with sneakers and a gray sweatshirt with The Wreck's logo printed across the front. Her long hair is piled into a messy bun on top of her head.

"C'mon, Kie, can't you do better than soda?" JJ complains, finally shifting his attention from the Kooks back to us. Kie holds her hands to her lips, shushing him. The plastic cups are full of beer, not soda. Kie winks.

"Dad said I could take a break and eat with you guys."

"Thought your dad didn't know we were here," I say.

Kiara collapses dramatically into the seat next to mine. "Nothing much gets past him," she says with a shrug. I offer her some of my chowder, but she shakes her head. "You kind of lose your taste for it after serving up hundreds of bowlfuls," she explains.

"More for me," I say, eating another delicious spoonful. I'm not sure I've ever been more hungry. My body is stiff and sore, but I already feel better than I did a few hours ago.

"How much longer until spring break is over?" Kie moans, lifting her arms above her head to stretch, revealing a strip of her taut stomach above the waistband of her jeans.

"Six days," Pope says, and Kie grins at me, because Pope didn't realize it was a rhetorical question. "What do you guys want to do for the rest of break?"

"I thought you had homework." JJ tries to make his voice sound serious, but I can tell he's trying not to laugh. The return of his sense of humor is a good sign.

Pope shrugs. "Finished it."

"Already?" JJ asks incredulously. "How will you fill your days without teachers to give you assignments?"

"Shut up." Pope shoves JJ playfully.

"Hey!" I shout. "He's already spilled chowder on my jacket. Let's not add beer to the equation."

Kiara reaches out to clap her hand over my mouth. "Soda, you mean," she corrects.

"Right, soda," I agree, my lips brushing against her palm when I speak. Despite the cool weather, Kie's skin is warm. For some reason, that makes me shiver.

I see Sarah Cameron and her boyfriend, Topper—back from Vail or wherever he was—joining the long table where Savannah and Hunter are sitting. Hunter and Topper do that handshake–chest bump thing that guys like them do. They must know each other somehow—maybe their parents belonged to the same country club or went to the same boarding school or something.

Or maybe Kooks just sort of fit together, no matter where they're from.

Sarah looks only slightly less bored here than she did the first night of spring break, eating dinner at the hotel with her parents. I remember how disappointed she was not to be in Aspen or Paris or wherever. Still, she helped us get out of there in one piece (more or less). She's wearing jeans and an oversized sweater, and her always-slightly-messy blond hair is long and loose down her back and tucked behind her ears. Topper's wearing shorts and flip-flops with a Patagonia fleece on top, only half dressed for the actual weather. His sunglasses are pushed to the top of his head, and his face is tanned, I guess from skiing or snowboarding or whatever. Sarah notices me looking at her and I politely smile a quick hello. I think I catch her smiling back, just for a second.

JJ said he thought Savannah was playing us last night. I'm not sure if he really believes that, or if he's just telling himself that to feel better about the fact that she chose to go back to her boyfriend instead of being with him. Anyway, I don't think Savannah was playing us so we'd help her last night. I think people are more complicated than that. Like, those smugglers threatened my life, and they obviously break the law selling hot electronics (and who knows what else)—but they also have families whose pictures they hang over their beds. Like Kie would say, the world isn't divided neatly into good guys or bad guys.

Even pirates.

Maybe even Kooks.

I gaze out past the docks to the ocean in the distance. I wonder if my dad would agree with me about good guys and bad guys. I wonder if he'd admonish me for nearly stealing that nav system or tease me for not moving fast enough to get it. For all the time we spent together on the water over the years, all the things he taught me about fishing and boating, there's so much I don't know about him. Does he hate Kooks like JJ does? Or does he think that no one is all good or all bad like Kie?

When he comes back home, I'm going to ask him.

"Come on, guys," Pope prompts. "I rushed to get my assignment done as quick as I could so that we'd have time to hang out, and you're all just staring off into space."

"Liar," I correct. "You've never rushed an assignment in your life."

Pope grins. "Okay, so maybe it just didn't take me as long as I thought it would, but still. Now I have the rest of spring break to do something with you guys. Another fishing trip, maybe?"

"No way," JJ and I say simultaneously. I laugh.

"Should we sneak into a different hotel?" Kiara suggests. "I have my maid's uniform ready to go," she adds with a wink. Sometimes I think Kie likes messing with the Kooks even more than the rest of us, like she's trying to prove to us that no matter how much money her family has, no matter where she lives, she's not *really* one of them.

"Nah-uh," JJ answers quickly. "I'm not stepping within ten feet of a Kook for the rest of spring break. Far as I'm concerned, Figure 8 is off-limits."

"Dude, you're sitting, like, two feet from a whole bunch of Kooks right now," Pope points out.

"He was a lot closer than that a couple nights ago," I start, but JJ's face darkens, and I know I can't make fun of him about Savannah, at least not yet. Maybe not ever.

Figure 8 isn't the only thing that's off-limits.

JJ shouts, "Screw the Kooks! Pogues forever!"

Most of the rich kids at the long table look at us like we're speaking gibberish. Savannah acts like she can't hear JJ at all. But I think I catch Sarah Cameron smiling again.

Yeah, I definitely don't think the world is divided into good guys and bad guys. Just from a numbers perspective, there have got to be some good Kooks out there. Maybe I've already met some and I don't know it yet.

But I don't think JJ is interested in shades of gray at the moment. He needs me to hate Savannah and the rest of them as much as he does. And however wild JJ and his schemes may be, he's my best friend. Sure, maybe it was his fault that we got caught in the storm the other night, but I know he wanted to get out on the water because he thought it would cheer me up, take my mind off . . . things. Besides, if I have to be stranded out on the water with someone, there's no one I'd rather be stranded with than JJ.

And then I realize something: JJ was never really intruding on "family time" when we were kids, showing up for all those fishing trips with me and my dad.

JJ was *becoming* my family.

Years ago, Dad told me that JJ and I had to take care of each other. JJ and I risked our lives for each other out there, and I know without a doubt that both of us would do it again if we had to.

Like I said, we're family.

I miss my dad, and I want him back. And I wish my uncle Teddy would stick around long enough that the Department of Child Services would stop sniffing around the Chateau. But until my dad gets back, I'm not *really* alone. I've got a family: JJ, Kie, Pope. They haven't left me; maybe they never will. I'd do anything for them. JJ and I said rough things to each other one minute and were laughing the next. We risked our lives for each other, no questions asked. Even after we fought with each other, we knew that when it really mattered, we were on the same side.

And Pope—we tease him about prioritizing school over everything else, but when we need him, he doesn't hesitate. He's the one who calmed JJ down when he was shadowboxing across my backyard yesterday. He's the one who can solve almost any problem. If I'd managed to snag that nav system, Pope would be poring over nautical maps alongside me, searching for my dad. Yes, even if it meant delaying his homework.

And Kie. She barely lasted a year at school with the Kooks before she came back to us. Pope couldn't believe she was passing up what her parents called a "world-class education," but Kie has her priorities straight.

The four of us, we'd do anything for one another. Break any stupid rules to be together. Forgive each other for almost anything.

What is that, if not a family?

So I lift my cup and reach across the table to knock it against JJ's. Just a little bit more quietly than JJ, I echo, "Screw the Kooks. Pogues forever."

Pope and Kiara follow suit. All four of us say it together, beers raised overhead.

Screw the Kooks. Pogues forever.

Acknowledgments

Heartfelt thanks to the kind and talented people who were instrumental in this book's creation: Brenda E. Angelilli, Lola Bellier, Laura Bernier, Shannon Burke, Matt Cramer, Mollie Glick, Jessica Gotz, Anne Heltzel, Joe Lawson, Kathy Lovisolo, Darice Murphy, Jonas Pate, Josh Pate, Hallie Patterson, Alex Rice, Brooke Shearouse, Andrew Smith, Matt Taylor, Amy Vreeland.

Thank you, JP Gravitt, for everything.

***

He couldn't remember how it felt to live his life without his dog.

—Alice Hoffman, *The Red Garden*